Praise for *Sanguine and Stygian*

"It's hard to even put how much I love this book into words. It's intense, steamy, and had such a great dark fantasy vibe."

-Amazon Reviewer

"Hands down one of the best fantasy romances out there."

-CJ Connor

"This book grips you from the beginning and doesn't let go. From the opening scene to the last sentence, you are wanting more. You just have to find out what happens next, and suddenly it's 2AM and you have to get up for work in 4 hours! Action, intrigue, magic, and romance!"

-Amazon Reviewer

"From the first page, you dive into this amazing fantasy realm full of magic & mercenaries. Fast paced with great characters and steamy romance scenes, you won't be able to put this book down.

-Bridget K. Shapiro

"Good luck sleeping! You won't want to put this one down. Action packed and full of heat and intrigue, you'll love the merry band of bawdy characters from start to finish… this book will whet your appetite for much more."

-Amazon Reviewer

THE STYGIAN CROWN

SARA SELLERS

Paperback ISBN: 978-1-7372194-3-9

Cover Design by Ravven
www.ravven.com

Map Art by Z
www.twitter.com/xy01011010

www.sarasellers.com

To all the authors who inspired me and lit up my childhood.
I couldn't have done it without you.

Also by Sara Sellers

The Sanguine and Stygian Series:

Sanguine and Stygian

Standalone Books:

The Storm King

TELERIA
Holy Forest of Whitefall
Mount Balmora
Karashae Desert
Balmoran Mountains
Widow's Fall
Mudbottom
Blackshear Forest
Liore
Raven's Rest
Blackhearth
Innistown
Temodor
The Black Hills
Portswell
Midburn
Lerathil
Travincal
Espyr

PROLOGUE

Logan palmed the letter between his fingers. It was worn down and wrinkled from how many times he'd read it, crumpled it up, then straightened it back out again over the past month. The paper was streaked orange from desert dust. He should have burned it a long time ago, but it kept pulling him back. He couldn't get her out of his head. Part of him wished he'd never read it.

I shudder to write this, but you deserve an explanation for my disappearance. Leaving you is the last thing I want to do right now. The Sanguine prisoner you've been holding is my brother, Wesley. The one I was searching for when I joined your clan and the closest thing to family I have left in this world. I hope you'll understand my deception. I can't let you hand him back to Victus. We've been through enough pain already.

I know you won't let us go easily. I beg of you, don't search for us. I need to help him start a new life away from the clans, however long that may take. I hope to one day return to the Brotherhood, once my brother is safe. I hope to return to you. I will miss you to my very marrow, Logan Vakarian.

Yours,

Kara

P.S. Sorry for drugging you.

LOGAN CRUSHED the paper in his fist.

CHAPTER ONE

One month earlier

"Do you really have to go?" Kara asked, tracing the whorls of dark hair on Logan's chest. She sprawled naked on top of him, one leg hooked around his as he cradled her in the crook of his arm.

"I have to rejoin the rest of the clan. They expected me a week ago."

"And you still can't tell me what the mission is?" Logan had negotiated another contract for the Stygians, one that took him away from the palace in Lerathil, but he refused to share the details of it with her.

His eyebrows knit together. "Classified, I'm afraid. It's safer if you don't know."

Kara closed her eyes and sighed against his skin. "Are you going to be gone longer than a month?" She hated the question, hated what it meant. Afraid to hear his answer.

"I'll make it back in time. For both of us."

"But what if you don't?" The keening would come for them both regardless.

"I'll be back, Kara."

"There you go again, making promises you can't keep." She hoped she was wrong.

"I don't make that promise lightly," he said, a low growl in his throat.

"And while you're away, I'm to fake being a noble and spy on members of the Lerathilian court. Without your help. No pressure."

"You'll do fine. Serena will help you. Just don't do anything I wouldn't do," he said, a wry grin spreading across his face. "Now, enough of goodbyes. We still have tonight." Logan flipped her beneath him in one smooth motion and pinned her down, his great muscular body stretching out over hers. He dipped his head to her neck and nibbled at her collarbone until she shrieked, then caught her scream between his lips.

"I'm going to miss this," Kara whispered between hard, frantic kisses. She wrapped her legs around him and pulled his hips toward hers until the hard heat of him rubbed between the crux of her thighs.

Logan hissed between his teeth. "Goddess, me too."

◖◗

THEY GOT little sleep that night, and the following morning Kara escorted Logan to the stable yard, the dark circles beneath her eyes hidden deep within the hood of her cloak. She squinted and winced at the sudden sunlight as they exited the castle's side door. They'd spent all their time since she'd healed from her encounter with Cervus and the Sanguines in the same removed set of halls and rooms beneath the servant's quarters, so far from the center of the castle that even the servants rarely trod them. At least her new identity would mean freedom, of a sort.

Kara's eyes adjusted to the light slowly. The palace

stables were constructed of ornate stone and curving arch-ways, and were large enough to hold a small army of horses. Dim-eyed stablehands led finely bred steeds with shining coats to their hitching posts to be saddled. Kara's hands fisted in the fabric of her cloak, a trickle of unease running through her. She felt out of place, and the game hadn't even begun. A stablehand appeared from an arch leading Char, who began to jerk his head and prance on the lead when he saw Logan.

"You better bring my horse back with you, Vakarian." Her mare, Drum, was still with the rest of the Stygian clan, wherever they were.

Logan laughed. "Of course, my lady."

Kara winced at the honorific.

Logan pulled her toward him and found her face within the cloak's hood, grasping her cheeks in his hands. "No goodbyes. I'll see you soon." He tilted her head up to kiss her, and his lips were desperate and hungry when they met hers. They said farewell, even if he wouldn't. She wrapped her hands around his neck and clashed her lips with his, tasting him. The spicy flavor of his blood danced on her tongue, and Kara realized she'd nicked his lip with her teeth.

Logan groaned and pulled her to him, crushing her in a tight embrace.

She buried her face in his neck and breathed deep, trying to capture the smell of him for safekeeping.

"Stay safe, little spitfire," he whispered.

"You too, Logan."

And then he was gone, striding towards Char and mounting in one smooth motion. He nodded to her once, and Kara tried to sear how he looked now, hair out of place and lips red from her brutal kisses, into her mind. And then he was galloping away.

The hole in Kara's chest spread, threatening to collapse.

Someone coughed, and Kara followed the noise. Serena leaned against an imposing stone column to the right, her dark hair framing her olive face and expressive brown eyes. Her hair was loose, and she was dressed in a simple cream blouse and leather breeches.

"Don't worry, he'll be back. He's got that look in his eye."

Kara quickly snuffed the flame of jealousy that threatened to rear its head. There was nothing between Serena and Logan now besides tense friendship, and the woman had saved her life on multiple occasions.

"Are you ready to begin?"

"Yes." Staying busy would distract her from missing the other half of her heart.

"Then follow me, my lady."

Kara stilled. The title was going to take some getting used to. Serena led her back through a different entrance into an unfamiliar wing of the castle. She struggled to keep from gawking at her surroundings. White marble floors covered in royal blue carpet runners led to an imposing split staircase at the head of the room. An enormous crystal chandelier dangled overhead, catching sunlight from the windows and refracting it. The entrance hall was flanked by statues carved into creatures of legend—a siren, her face contorted in ecstasy as she was swallowed by a wave. A horse with wings that spanned ten feet across, each feather wrought in glorious detail. Kara traced her hand over a wingtip, running the pads of her fingers across the individual barbs.

"It takes some getting used to," Serena said.

Kara drug her eyes from one extravagance to another as she followed Serena up the marble steps. She hated that she thought it was beautiful. The second story featured endless hallways and doors leading to an untold number of rooms. Portraits of royalty hung on the walls, their austere gazes staring down at her.

Serena stopped in front of a room at the end of the hall and opened the door, ushering her in. "Your new quarters."

The room wasn't as garish as the one she'd stayed in at Baroness Valancourt's in Travincal, thank the goddess, but it was still uncomfortably lavish. A fire blazed in the hearth, which was carved out of the same white stone as the statues. Gold and grey veins streaked through the marble and splintered out across the mantelpiece. A bed large enough for three people sat in front of the fire. It was dressed in stark white linens, and a diaphanous blue curtain hung from the four-poster canopy, flowing down to the floor. Kara wanted to climb into the bed and shut herself inside the curtain for a while.

Serena strode past the bed to a walnut-colored armoire and snapped open the doors, revealing a dark green gown beaded with white pearls. "Put this on. I'm taking you to meet the king."

"Excuse me?" Kara's jaw hung slack.

"We need to hammer out the details of your employment, and he wants to meet you before you begin."

Serena passed her the gown, and Kara stood there, clenching the heavy fabric. "This is all happening very quickly."

"If you can navigate Vakarian, you can navigate anyone. You'll do fine." Serena opened a drawer in the armoire and began chucking pieces of white fabric onto the bed, including stockings, a slip, and a corset.

"Who am I pretending to be?" Kara laid the gown on the bed and began to undress.

"Lady Celine Grey, newly come to court in search of a husband."

Kara paused, her shirt halfway over her head. "*What?*"

"It's the best cover. You can bond with the other debutantes or attend soirees with their mothers, and it will allow you to get close to any single men you're investigating without raising suspicion."

"Mother Night. Did Logan know about this plan?"

"What do you think?" Serena asked, arching an eyebrow.

Kara sighed. "And is Lady Celine real?"

"No, but Robert Grey, the Lord of Briarcliff, is, and he's in hot water with King Calim. He doesn't come to court often, and his estate is remote enough that people shouldn't be too suspicious at your sudden appearance. I'll leave it to you if you want to be public about being marked or not. This is Lerathil, so everyone's got a Namirahn somewhere in the family tree. You'll find judgmental assholes all over Teleria, but by and large you wouldn't be scorned for it."

What would it be like to not be judged for her curse? She'd had a taste of that with Logan and the Brotherhood, but now she was wearing a mask again. Kara donned the undergarments and stepped into the dress, unused to the feel of such soft fabric against her skin. She pulled it up and pushed her arms through the sleeves, then turned so Serena could help her lace up the corset and gown.

Serena tackled the laces with deft fingers. "You'll have a lady's maid to help you with this most of the time. You can reach her with the bell-pull by the bed."

"I don't need a maid in my business when I'm trying to spy."

"Well I have duties other than lacing up your dresses," Serena said, yanking the laces taut. "And unless you learned to do your hair like a Countess's daughter from Philipe Galois, you're going to need her."

Serena finished lacing her up, and Kara pinned her hair up in a simple twist. Countess's daughter or not, it would have to do for now.

Serena took a step back and looked her over. "You clean up nice, McKenna. Calim is going to eat his teeth."

Kara slid on a pair of ivory slippers and followed Serena back to the first floor, then down several sidehalls. Serena navigated the labyrinthine palace with confidence, but Kara was beginning to doubt her ability to find her way back to her room without getting turned around.

They entered a room behind a tall set of double doors, and Kara sucked in a breath. Bookshelves lined the room, stretching two stories high. Rolling ladders rested against the bookshelves, and several spiral staircases led to a floating walkway that bordered the second level of books. Fae lanterns bobbed along the second-floor banister, teasing passerby to peek over the edge.

Against the far walls, three enormous hearths blazed with glowing green fire, like the cavernous maws of some many-mouthed beast.

"Spellfires. So the smoke won't damage the books and there's no chance of an actual fire spreading." Serena locked the library doors behind them. "There are reading rooms here, if you ever need a break. Though they're mainly used for illicit rendezvous. Come, the king awaits."

Kara followed Serena's gaze to the library's sole occupant. A man reclined in a plush leather chair, a book in his hands and reading glasses halfway down his nose. He wore an unassuming doublet in royal blue and black breeches tucked into tall boots. A plate of half-eaten lemon cookies sat on the end table beside him. He wore no circlet or crown, though Kara supposed she would not want to wear a crown all the time either, were she queen.

Kara approached him and executed one of the slow, graceful curtsies Philipe had trained her to do by making her balance a book on her head. "Your highness."

The king glanced up at her and recoiled, dropping his book in his lap. Then he shook his head and met her eyes again, closing the cover with trembling fingers. "Apologies. You look a lot like someone I know."

The king's close-cropped brown hair was greying at the temples, his eyes a warm chocolate color. The lack of royal seals or jewelry on his person, not even a ring, surprised Kara. Was he as humble as his wardrobe?

Calim motioned for her to rise. "You must be Vakarian's girl." He had the crisp consonants and polished accent of an aristocrat.

Kara tried not to let her annoyance show on her face. "I'm my own person."

Had his lips twitched at that?

"Of course, forgive me. Where are you from, again? I won't ask your name—best to forget it ever existed while you're here."

"The Balmoran Mountains."

Calim took off his reading glasses and cleaned them with his sleeve, a thoughtful expression on his face. "Interesting. You don't look like mountain stock."

"I was adopted."

Calim's eyes flickered to Serena, then settled on Kara's face, analyzing. "Impressive, seeker. I could almost believe we were related."

Serena smirked, settling onto the couch across from Calim and crossing her legs. Kara was unsure if it'd be rude to sit in his presence, but Calim gestured for her to take the chair next to him.

"What's your education like? Vakarian didn't give me much to go on."

Best not to tell him a soldier turned farrier had home-schooled her. Kara shrugged. "Just a village school in the north. I can read and write and do sums, but they rarely got philosophical. Philipe Galois of Travincal taught me etiquette and dancing, though. I can blend in in the ballroom."

"Well, you came highly recommended. Vakarian doesn't give praise lightly, and I trust him and Serena. Shall we talk business?"

Kara nodded. "I'd like to discuss my pay." She needed the money to come to her, not the Stygians, since she wasn't sure how quickly the dustup over her breaking Wesley out of their safehouse would settle once they returned.

Calim broke into a grin. "Of course. A mercenary's favorite topic. You'll be generously compensated for every week you remain in my employ. There will be bonuses for any information you bring me that proves useful in identifying the Sanguine sympathizers. Find out which nobles are in their pockets. Since it's a Stygian contract, will you be giving Vakarian his cut? Or do I need to set it aside for him?"

Kara smiled, and it was all teeth. "I'll give it to him." *Once I'm accepted back into the clan.*

"All your expenses will be taken care of," Serena said. "I've made you an appointment with the best modiste in the city already. Is your room to your satisfaction?"

Kara nodded. "Do you have any leads on the Sanguine threat? Where do I start?"

"To begin with, familiarize yourself with the palace and the courtiers in residence," Calim said. "Try to find your way into their good graces. There's new information that's come to light since I negotiated this contract, though."

"What is it, your highness?"

"Please. I'm just a man with a crown. Call me Calim."

Kara gulped. How in Teleria had she ended up here, with the king of the realm, being told to call him by his first name? It struck her anew that she was talking to the grandson of Urian, the man partially responsible for the creation of Namirah's curse.

"Calim." His name stuck in her throat.

"We believe there's a threat to my sister, Princess Ariana's, life."

"From the Sanguines?"

Calim nodded. "That's our suspicion. Ariana's betrothal to the Prince of Gavroche will be announced soon. Their marriage stands to strengthen the crown in both trade and military might, make us a real contender in Teleria again. There are some who'd prefer we remain weak."

"The Vespertines will protect her," Serena said, "but people know who we are. They see us coming, know our habits and schedules. You, however… You don't have to be by her side day and night, but we'd like to you look out for danger. And find the person plotting to kill her before it's too late."

"My sister and I are the last in line to the throne. We have no heirs. We must dig out the roots of dissidence, or the problem will fester and grow. The palace is large, but our army is small. If the Sanguines took Lerathil, or, goddess forbid, instilled their own puppet monarch on the throne, I don't think even the guild could stop them. Or the Stygians," he said pointedly.

Kara's mind whirled. Hunting a princess's assassin sounded like a good way to end up dead. It'd be lucrative, though…and Logan or no Logan, she needed to secure her own money with her status with the Stygians still in limbo.

"Where is Princess Ariana right now?"

"She went to find herself in the desert," Serena said, "but she'll be returning soon. Her ladies-in-waiting would be a good place to start. They have powerful spouses, men who always tend to want more. You'll need to be in their good graces if you want to get any information out of them."

"And will the princess know my true identity?"

Calim faltered, and his eyes darted to Serena's again. "For now, no. We'll inform her if it becomes important. Are you up to the job?"

Kara nodded. "I'll take it."

Calim's face broke into a beaming smile. "Splendid. My sister's due to return to court soon, and I've been planning a masque to celebrate her return. Many foreign officials and dignitaries, as well as some of our own diplomats, will be there. Hopefully you'll feel at home in the palace by then and will be able to gather some information."

CHAPTER TWO

Kara got lost twice on her way back to her room, and when she finally found it, she was exhausted and overwhelmed. A headache pulsed at her temples, threatening to grow. She fell face-down into the soft bed and groaned when she realized she'd need help to unlace this blasted gown.

There was a gentle knock on the door. "Come in," she moaned, assuming it was Serena.

A young woman with mousy brown hair pulled into a sleek bun entered and immediately curtsied, her nose nearly scraping the floor. Kara rolled to her feet, waiting for the girl to rise and introduce herself, but she continued to hold the position. *Bugger.*

"Ah, please rise."

"Pleased to make your acquaintance, my lady. I'm Merry," the girl said. Her eyes were a clear, pale blue, her collarbones sharp beneath her plain dress.

Kara was tempted to say *good for you,* but decided not to rile the girl. "I'm—"

"Oh, I know who you are, of course, Lady Grey. They told me you were coming weeks ago. I've been eagerly awaiting your arrival."

Weeks? Logan must have been planning for her to take this contract since before she'd fled with Wesley. *Yet he never mentioned it to me.* That man needed to learn to be less withholding.

Merry frowned at Kara's pinched expression. "Shall I draw you a bath, my lady?"

"That sounds divine. Where are the baths located?"

Merry smiled and made her way across the room, where she pressed a wooden panel on the wall that swung open. A hidden door. "There's a tub in the antechamber."

Kara raised her eyebrows. An attached bathroom? Her very own tub? What had she done to deserve this? She crossed the bedroom and resisted the urge to whistle when she followed Merry into the bathing chamber. A tub made of clear glass sat in the center of the room, flanked by a sink fixture and a tall oval mirror ringed with silver filigree.

Several braided silk ropes hung beside the head of the tub, and three runes were etched into the bottom of the clear glass.

"Are you familiar with water runes?"

"No," Kara said, trying to keep the awe out of her voice.

"Red silk for hot water, blue for cold. Black for an evaporation spell."

"I think I'm in love."

Merry giggled. It relieved Kara to see a crack in her shell.

Kara spotted a matching set of runes and silk ropes by the sink. She tugged the red rope experimentally, and warm water filled the bowl, as if it seeped in from the glass itself. She suppressed a squeal of delight. "Can you please help me with my dress?"

"Of course, Lady Grey." Merry swiftly undid the laces of the dress and corset, and Kara let them drop in a puddle at her feet. She stepped out of the circle of clothes and pulled her slip overhead, then started on the stockings.

Merry gasped. Kara's eyes flew to her left wrist, but her silver cuff was still in place, hiding Namirah's curse mark. Had her scars surprised her?

Merry averted her eyes as she bent to pick up the dress, her cheeks a bright pink.

"Apologies, Merry. Modesty isn't an affliction I suffer from." She must be new to ladysmaiding if she was unaccustomed to people undressing in front of her.

"No worries, my lady. You just surprised me. Will you require anything else of me this evening?"

"You're free to go. Thank you for your help."

Merry curtsied and scurried away, and Kara heard her hanging the dress up in the armoire before the bedroom door snicked shut.

Kara experimented with the ropes and filled the tub until she had water that was almost too hot to stand, then sunk into it with a sigh. She leaned her head back against the rim, wishing Logan was here to massage her neck and head until her headache vanished and she melted in his arms.

She imagined he was here, sneaking into the bathroom and diving his hands beneath the water to touch her. Imagined he was in the bedroom beyond, standing naked in front of the fire, waiting for her to finish her bath to take her into his arms. Imagined he was anywhere but gone.

()

Kara accompanied Serena to the palace training yards in the morning. Apparently the Vespertines, the palace guard, and what little of the royal army remained stationed here trained together often. She hadn't been able to practice regularly since the clan had left for Travincal, and she sorely missed it. Exercise was one of the ways she kept the volatility of the curse under control. Serena loaned her clothes to wear after Kara accepted her invitation. To Kara's surprise, she'd said it wasn't uncommon for the women of the court to join the sessions, either for exercise or to learn self-defense. Kara was relieved to be in a pair of pants again, even if they were embroidered with a filigree.

A tall man with straight blond hair and piercing blue eyes approached Kara as she stretched her legs on the training yard green. He bowed low to her. She tilted her head up to get a better look at him. He was handsome, with a chiseled jaw, aquiline nose, and bronze skin. His tan breeches hugged muscular thighs, and the vee of his green shirt revealed a dusting of blond hair. *A target appears.*

"Welcome to Lerathil, Lady Grey. We've been eagerly awaiting your arrival. I'm Viscount Kendrick. But you can call me Aidan." Serena must have planted the seeds of her arrival far in her advance, as no one seemed surprised by her sudden appearance.

"Kendrick?" Kara paused, scouring her brain. Why did that sound so familiar? Then it clicked into place. *Jasper!* That was his last name.

"Do you have a brother, Aidan?"

"Several. Have you had the misfortune of meeting one of them?"

Kara smiled. She'd have to judge Aidan on his own merits. "I've heard talk, is all."

"Count yourself lucky, then."

Aidan dropped into a stretch beside her, and the court ladies that'd been chatting on a bench nearby quickly rose and came closer, beginning their own stretches as they watched him.

Kara chuckled under her breath. "It appears you have an audience."

Aidan glanced up. "Ah. I've grown inured to it. Do you spar regularly, Lady Grey?"

"Please, call me Celine. And I do, from time to time. I enjoyed many outdoor activities in the country."

"I've been to Briarcliff. The land there is wild and beautiful."

Shit. She needed to be careful about bringing up the earl or Briarcliff before she had the opportunity to learn more about them. "But not so beautiful as the palace, of course."

"If you say so. I find I prefer the ruggedness of country living as I age. Pray tell, what tempted you out of it?"

"The threat of spinsterhood."

Aidan cracked a smile, transforming his face. Kara blinked at him. No one should look that good while touching their toes. She was beginning to understand what the ladies of the court had lined up for.

"And you? What brings you to the palace?"

"I command a portion of the royal army that's stationed here."

Kara forgot herself for a moment when she said, "For a man so fond of nature, you seem to have chosen the wrong profession."

Surprise flickered across his face. "Indeed. Army outposts grow fewer as mercenary control spreads. But you're familiar with that, with your borders so close to Dreadnettle's."

Kara nodded. "They certainly contribute to the wildness. Perhaps you can retire to a hermitage." She finished stretching and dusted her hands off on her pants. As a captain in the army, Aidan seemed unlikely to be a Sanguine sympathizer. But honor often knelt to coin. And he *was* related to Jasper.

"You must be an accomplished swordsman. Would you care to spar?"

"I wouldn't want to hurt you—"

"Nonsense. You insult me, my lord."

"Very well, Celine." The way her new name rolled off his lips was seductive.

Kara caught Serena's eye as she and the viscount took up practice swords. The mage was in the middle of a cluster of Vespertines, giving them instructions for their workout.

She and Aidan began slowly, going through a set pattern of attacks and deflections. His gaze was bored, unfocused. His eyes flitted between the other groups of people around the yard. Kara gave him a quick rap on the collarbone to wake him up.

"I said I wanted to spar, not trade blows like children." Kara deviated from the pattern again, darting in to give him a cheeky poke to his inner thigh. She was going to have to threaten him to get him to take her seriously. Aidan deflected the swift blows she followed up with, his eyes widening.

"You're fast. Who did you train with?"

Keep it vague, Kara. "The man who taught me to ride was an excellent swordsman."

"And you an excellent student." Aidan began to duel her in earnest, increasing his speed and varying his blows, though she sensed he was still holding back. If he'd trained with the same tutor Jasper had, he'd be quite the swordsman.

The thudding of the wooden practice swords meeting soothed her with their brutal lullaby. She almost missed the feeling of Aethyta's gaze on her back, the clap of her hands ringing in the air. A pang went through her as she wished Jon or Logan were here to spar with. They always challenged her.

A few of the Vespertines gathered around, watching them fight. Kara wanted to show off her full skills to impress them, but she controlled herself, pulling her swings and letting Aidan score hits she'd have normally blocked or dodged.

They continued for several more minutes, then Kara pulled off, acting winded. She could slowly escalate Celine's abilities and stamina, just as she had her own. She might already be pushing it.

She wiped sweat off her brow and smiled at Aidan. "I'm afraid I'm spent. Thank you for humoring me."

"Any time, my lady. Your skills are impressive. I look forward to our next bout."

Kara paused. Aidan may be able to give her more information on the situation at the palace, but she'd need to be alone with him if she wanted him to be candid with her.

"Could I interest you in giving me a tour around Lerathil sometime, Lord Kendrick? I have had little chance for tourism, and you must know the city well." Kara had no memory of her trip into the city, when Logan had rushed her to the castle as she bled out. The heads of the court ladies twisted around like owls, listening in. This wouldn't win her any fans amongst them—Kendrick was obviously a hotly contested bachelor.

Aidan blushed. "Of course, Celine. It'd be my pleasure."

()

THAT EVENING, Kara and Serena went on a ride around the castle grounds, which extended beyond the palace proper and encapsulated a section of Lerathil's rolling green countryside. Kara was given a fine mare from the stables to use, which made her miss Drum all the more.

It was the first chance she'd had to get a good look at the palace from a distance. Its seven white spires pierced the sky, each peaked with blue slate tiles. High white walls surrounded the palace, separating it from the city below. The scenery was beautiful, the air crisp without being cold, and Kara had every material thing she could ever want at her beck and call. Yet she still felt ill at ease.

"Thank you for inviting me to the training yard today. I needed it."

"I figured you were probably getting antsy, being cooped up in the castle the last few weeks."

Logan had kept her plenty entertained, but Kara didn't think Serena would appreciate that knowledge.

"My offer still stands, you know. To join the Vespertines."

Kara swung her head towards Serena. "Really?"

"Why not? You're smart. And a brilliant fighter."

Sometimes Kara wondered what the past year would've been like had she taken Serena up on her offer, back during the Reaping Trials. But the Brotherhood was part of her now, even if she wasn't part of it.

"Things are still…in limbo, regarding my contract with the Stygians. I need to see that through before making any decisions."

"Well, keep us in mind. The mercenary life is hard, and the women in the Vespertines are a good sort. I'll introduce you at the next training session."

As Celine. Which meant their relationship would begin on a lie.

"Speaking of training, I don't know that Kendrick will be of much help with the Sanguines, unless you're just looking to get your mind off Vakarian."

Kara snorted. "As if that's possible."

Serena snapped her head back and laughed. "Oh, I don't miss *that* feeling. What's bothering you?"

Kara smiled at her. The mage was fast becoming a good friend and her sole confidante at the palace.

"The man's impossible. I don't know what we are, what I mean to him—if he just sees this as temporary or something more."

"And you never will, unless he's changed."

"I wish he would tell me the things he says with his body. That he'd trust me more. I don't know what he's so afraid of." *That you'll betray him again,* her mind whispered.

"Probably the same things you are."

"How did you deal with it, when things ended between you?"

"Ours was no great love story, Kara. I broke things off between us."

"What? Really?" Someone had dumped Logan Vakarian? Kara's esteem for Serena grew.

"He was never there, even when we were together. Not really. I'd look in his eyes, and he'd be a thousand miles away. Plus I've got some commitment issues of my own."

"If you'd rather not talk about this, please tell me."

"You're fine. I'd like to help. My advice? Don't wait for him. I worry that you'll get hurt if you do. The clan has always been first in his heart. You're young, beautiful, deadly with an assortment of weapons. What's not to like? There are plenty of other men out there."

Men who don't know the real me. Men who, if they did, would look at me in fear and disgust, or as a curiosity to be sampled. Logan saw the beast inside her and didn't flinch, because that beast lived in him, too.

"However…" Serena started, and Kara looked up at her. "When he brought you to me, on the brink of death—I've never seen him so rattled. And Vakarian doesn't rattle easily. Nor does he promise favors, *ever*, and he promised one for you. I'm no romantic, but that must mean something, Kara." Serena reached down and patted her horse's neck. "So, you'll probably destroy each other or live happily ever after."

Kara barked out a laugh. *Why not both?*

"I don't think I've thanked you properly for saving my life, by the way."

"You wouldn't have made it to me if Logan hadn't cast a blood spell on you. A very dangerous and forbidden spell, by the way."

"Forbidden? Why?" She could recall the sweet copper taste of his blood in her mouth, the surge of warmth after he'd drawn the rune on her chest, but everything after was darkness.

"The sanguinata. Blood binding. He gave you his blood then bound it with yours, letting the power in his blood invigorate you."

Kara swallowed. "Is it…permanent?"

"I don't know."

"What makes it so dangerous? I've noticed no ill effects."

"Your blood could've been incompatible, causing your body to reject it. Or if you had died while his blood was still in your system, it could have weakened and killed him."

"*Oh.*" Logan had risked that for her? Had he known it was a possibility?

Serena paused, gazing out at the sunset blanketing the distant hills. Her horse lowered his head to grab a chomp of grass. "Do you want to see him?"

"Of course, but I've no idea where he is. He didn't deign to share that information."

"There might be a way. Come to my workshop tonight."

KARA FOLLOWED Serena to her workshop after they put the horses away. The grooms offered to take care of them, but Kara enjoyed the routine of unsaddling and brushing down a horse. It helped her center and calm herself.

Serena's workshop was in one of the palace's seven spires, atop an endless spiral staircase that reminded Kara of her old room at Raven's Rest. The last step opened into the workshop, opposite an arched window that gazed out over the city. The spires, lit by the moon and stars, were breathtaking to behold from this height. Why couldn't she have been born in a place as beautiful as this? Where the curse was so omnipresent that it seemed less a burden. Kara leaned out the window and looked down at the drop below—at the sheer height she was at—and imagined what it'd feel like to ride a rope pulley all the way to the ground. She could almost feel the wind rushing through her hair.

Kara turned back to Serena, who was reaching on her tip-toes to retrieve a plain-looking black bowl from a tall shelf. The room was lined with potions and crystals and weapons etched with runes, but despite all the things in it, it didn't feel cluttered. Everything had its place.

Serena brought the bowl over to the sink beside Kara. The inside of the bowl was carved with complicated, interlocking runes. Most runes Kara had seen were simple, like the ones etched to the bottom of her bathtub or stitched into Logan's cloak, but this looked like someone had knotted twenty runes together and arranged them in a symmetrical pattern.

Serena filled the bowl with warm water and placed it on the table in the center of the room. "A word to the wise regarding this bowl. Don't jump to conclusions. Now, look into it and think of the person you want to see. Focus on a strong, positive memory of them."

Serena stepped away to her work desk, and Kara stared into the water. She pictured Logan on the last night they'd been together, when he'd been content to lie beside her and trace the lines of her body with his fingertips, eyes dark with emotion.

The water grew cloudy, then an image wavered on its surface.

It was Logan, his skin sun-kissed and jaw thick with stubble. Kara resisted the urge to caress his image in the water. Wherever he was, the sun hadn't set yet. It wavered low on the horizon. The steady bob of his frame was consistent with someone riding a horse. The image in the water shifted, drawing back, and Kara frowned. A beautiful woman in blue silks rode beside him, laughing at something he said. She curled a possessive hand around Logan's bicep and pointed to something in the distance.

Kara tasted blood. She'd bitten her tongue, hard. There was something about the image that was nagging at her. The black horse the woman was riding looked familiar. Logan and the woman turned, and the horse's profile came into view. It was Drum. She was riding *her* horse!

Kara raked her fingers through the pool of water, distorting the image. It faded with a tingle.

"Shouldn't stick your hand in things you don't understand," Serena tsked.

"Does this bowl show the present?"

Serena nodded.

"I've seen enough."

"Are you sure?"

"Yes."

Kara regretted coming here, regretted asking the question she'd feared to have answered. She was risking her neck at the palace to get back in the clan's good graces, entirely out of her element, and he was gallivanting around goddess knows where with some woman. A woman riding *her* horse. Kara had never felt jealousy like this—this ragged clawing at the edges of her stomach. She should have made Logan clarify exactly what they were to each other before he left, but when he'd asked her to wait for him, she'd assumed that meant he'd wait for her, too.

Kara took a few deep breaths, trying to calm herself. It was only a hand, only a horse. She was overreacting. It could be entirely innocent, and he deserved an opportunity to explain himself.

"Uh oh. Amber eyes. What did you see?"

"Nothing good."

"You wanna talk about it?"

"Suffice it to say that you might have been right."

"Hmm. Sometimes I think that bowl's cursed."

"Do you spy on people with this all the time?"

"It's a lover's bowl. Only good for seeing people you have a deep bond with."

"Does the bond have to go both ways?"

Serena nodded. "Though I don't recommend it as a replacement for daisy-pulling. The bowl is much more fickle than that."

"Can I take it with me?" Kara already wanted to look into the bowl again, regretted disrupting the image. What if she missed something important?

"Will you use it responsibly?"

"Probably not."

"Don't torture yourself, Kara."

"Is that a yes?"

Serena sighed. "Fine. Just *don't* try to contact the dead. Trust me."

Kara poured the water out into the sink, and the runed stone quickly absorbed it. An odd idea wormed its way into her mind. "What happens if you fill the bowl with blood instead of water?"

Serena looked at her sharply. "Mother Night, what would even possess you to ask that? I don't know, and I wouldn't like to find out. I don't practice blood magic."

"Do you know someone who does? Logan told me I'd be able to use it eventually."

Serena frowned and chewed her lip. "There is another mage at the palace…a man named Salizar. I wouldn't choose him as your teacher, though."

"Why not?"

"Some people crave power so much that they have no respect for how they acquire it. There have been rumors among Namirah's Chosen at court lately. He's peddling a supposed antidote to the monthly keening."

Kara stalled, heart fluttering in her chest. "That exists?" Logan would have mentioned such an alternative to her, right?

Serena glanced at Kara and twisted her hands together. "Perhaps I shouldn't have told you of this. I doubt it works, Kara. He's still refining it, and some of the women have gotten sick from it. Besides, Salizar does nothing without an ulterior motive. Some things are better borne."

"You don't know what it's like, Serena. To lose control, lose yourself. If it works, that would be…"

Serena lowered her eyes. "You're right. It's your decision. Just be careful."

Kara caught Serena in a hug. The mage's body was stiff, arms at her side. She slowly relaxed and returned the embrace, gingerly patting Kara on the back.

"Thank you," Kara said.

CHAPTER THREE

Time, as it did most places, moved swiftly in Lerathil. Kara went to her appointment with the modiste that week. They draped her in fabric and poked her with stray pins for hours on end. The shop assistants presented her with swatches of fabric in a hundred different colors and textures, and Kara mostly went with her gut. The silk looked less scratchy than lace; she preferred darker, striking colors to pastels. The dressmaker complained about her 'breeding hips' and muscular arms multiple times, asking if she'd made a hobby of lifting bricks at Briarcliff. Kara left the shop exhausted, hungry, and lightly perforated.

Garments began to slowly arrive at the palace, and Merry filled up the armoire with them, gushing over the quality of the fabric and the stylish, if revealing, cuts. Serena's bowl was currently in the depth of that same armoire, burning a hole into Kara's brain. She fought the urge to look into it every night. Serena had warned her about jumping to conclusions, but Kara was afraid of what she might see if she looked again. Afraid to see something unmistakable.

Kara had to ask a palace guard for directions to Salizar's workshop. She'd expected it to be in one of the seven spires, like Serena's, but the guard directed her to the palace cellars. She followed a stone path off the kitchens that led through an extensive wine cellar and ended at the door to a circular chamber. Perhaps he liked his drink readily available.

Kara took a deep breath and knocked on the broad oak door to Salizar's workshop. She'd have to tell him she was marked, but hopefully he'd be discrete. She'd pay him off if she had to.

There was a curse from inside. A few minutes later, the door creaked open. The man who peered around it was younger than Kara expected, with tousled black hair that fell into his eyes and a sharp, straight nose. He was sallow-skinned, as if he rarely saw the sun, and his eyes were a striking pale green. Was he Salizar's assistant?

"Is Salizar in?"

"No, he's halfways out. Do I know you?"

The man himself. He looked to be in his twenties still, with an attractive, fine-boned face. She'd expected the creator of the antidote to be older. "I'm Lady Grey of Briarcliff."

Salizar laughed. "Of course you are. And how do you come to find yourself here, Lady Grey?"

Kara had grown accustomed to people bowing or curt-sying when they first met 'Lady Grey,' and when Salizar didn't, it unsettled her. Did he have suspicions about her true identity, or was he just rude? "Serena referred me. May I come in?"

Salizar glanced behind the door into his workshop, then slid his head back out. Something that smelled like burnt hair sizzled within. "I'm rather busy at the moment."

"I won't keep you long."

Salizar swung the door open and gestured her in. "Fine, fine. Do what you want."

Kara stepped inside the workshop, and Salizar rushed over to a teeming cauldron threatening to boil over—the source of the burnt hair smell—and began stirring it with a spoon the length of her leg.

"Close the door behind you," Salizar snapped. The dangling sleeves of his over-sized robe threatened to dip into the cauldron's contents as he stirred.

The workshop was badly in need of cleaning. Cobwebs clung to the dark stone walls and wooden rafters, and a fine layer of multicolor powders coated the floor. Merry was going to be displeased at the state of Kara's hemline.

The cauldron wasn't the only thing brewing and secreting smells. There was an elaborate array of lab equipment lining the far wall. Smoke bubbled atop beakers and flasks filled with brightly colored liquids, and thin rivulets of steam escaped from vibrating metal pots. Clear glass piping looped above the glassware, depositing drops of liquid that sputtered and smoked. Shelves studded every free wall in the room, teeming with jars that contained an assortment of macabre ingredients. Kara read the labels on the ones close to her—bitterweed, badger blood, widow's teeth. One jar held a human eyeball suspended in a clear jelly. The iris was the same deep red as Logan's when he was losing control to the curse. As Kara moved past it, the eyeball turned, tracking her movements. She shuddered, and a line of sweat began to form down her spine.

"Whose eye is that?"

"I can't say. It was donated to me."

Where would he get the living eye of a Namirahn? Victus?

"Have you just come to poke around in my things and gawk, then?"

"Serena told me you might have a way to suppress Namirah's curse, avoid the monthly toll."

Salizar looked up from his stirring, thick eyebrows raising. "I might. Who's asking?"

"I am." Kara unclasped the silver cuff on her left wrist and bared her mark to him.

Salizar smiled. "Well well, Lady Grey. Aren't you full of surprises? I didn't know you suffered from the curse. Then again, no one knows much of anything about you, do they?"

Kara stilled. Why was he so suspicious of her? Perhaps Calim had let something slip about her identity. "I don't like to advertise the fact. I'd appreciate it if we could keep it between the two of us."

"Of course, my lady. I have been…experimenting, lately, with varied results, on a potion that acts as a kind of block for the curse."

"How varied are these results?"

"No one's died yet." He grinned and licked his incisors. "A few of the court ladies come to me for it when they're having a lover's spat and would like to avoid keening for a month, but there's been little prolonged testing."

"And the side effects?" Serena had mentioned women falling ill.

"In order to block the negatives of the curse, one must also block the positives. I've yet to find a way around it. You will feel weaker because you'll be weaker. Your senses will be less heightened. You may find you get sick more easily. But some find those drawbacks well worth the sacrifice."

"I'd like a dose of it. As long as that's not it," she said, nodding towards the caustic contents of the cauldron. Kara had no plans to take the antidote yet, but she was curious to see if it actually worked. Not having the pressure to feed the curse slowly consume her thoughts each month would be a welcome relief. And she wouldn't be burdened by having to rely on someone else.

Salizar's eyes lit up. "Are you positive, my lady? I'm sure the king would be happy to have you execute some prisoners for him. Our executioner isn't even Namirahn— a waste, truly. Alternatively, the men at court are accustomed to being asked to service the keening of the court ladies."

Kara raised her eyebrows. He made it all sound so transactional. "I'd like to keep my options open. And I'm no killer." It wasn't *entirely* a lie. She'd much rather earn a kill in battle than be made to play executioner.

Salizar laughed like he didn't believe her. "Very well." He walked over to a row of frothing glass cylinders and plucked one full of bubbling black slime out, then poured it into a small vial. The substance sludged between containers, black tendrils gripping at the surface of the glass as if it were reluctant to leave. He stoppered the vial and handed it to her.

Of course it'd be the black, noxious liquid instead of the one that looked like strawberry cream.

"I've started calling it demon's drip."

Kara uncorked the vial and sniffed, wrinkling her nose at the sulfuric stench. She narrowed her eyes at Salizar. "What in the goddess's name is in this?"

"It requires blood from a variety of live specimens. Carefully extracted and boiled with a proper catalyst. Perhaps the most dangerous element is the highly vitriolic—"

Kara held up her hand before he could finish. "Stop. I changed my mind, I don't want to know. I don't have to drink this stuff, do I?" The potion had an inky black consistency that clouded the bottle and seemed to writhe about of its own volition.

Salizar shook his head and passed her a leather pouch with several glass syringes inside. "You *can* swallow it, or you may inject it into a vein—I'll leave it up to you. I'm told the taste is abominable. I must warn you, in its current state, the antidote is meant as a last resort, not a permanent solution. Some have an unpleasant reaction at first."

"Such as?"

"Your body will need time to adjust. You may vomit or suffer abdominal pain. You're not pregnant, right?"

"I'm not. How much is it?" Such things didn't come free. If he perfected it, he'd be a very rich mage. Maybe she could add it to her court expenses.

"While it's still undergoing testing, I'm not charging. I do ask a small favor of my customers though, to aid research and development."

Ah, the catch.

"I'd like a sample of your blood—before and after you take the potion—to study and compare. It's my hope that these samples will help me in refining the formula."

"How much blood?"

"A small vial full."

Kara hesitated. Namirahn blood held power. What would Salizar be able to do with hers, as a practitioner of blood magic? Could he use it to discover her true identity? And if he did, could she trust him to keep it a secret? He was one of Calim's court mages, but Kara wouldn't be here if everyone was loyal to the crown.

"I'll make you a deal."

"I'm listening," Salizar said as he adjusted dials on his

equipment, making the flame licking at one of his flasks shrink and expand in size.

"I'll give you my blood in exchange for a potion each month if you agree to teach me blood magic. All of Namirah's Chosen are capable of it, are they not?" Kara couldn't wait for Logan to teach her. There was danger afoot in the palace, and she needed every edge she could get.

Salizar's throat bobbed. "Yes, in theory there's enough latent power in your blood that it can fuel spells. But it's a dangerous art. What does an aristocratic girl like you need to know blood magic for?"

He was testing her, probing. "I'm so used to the curse controlling me… For once I'd like to control it. Use it for my own gain. I'm tired of living in fear."

"Fair enough. I'll do what I can, but blood magic takes years to master." He pulled a large black tome off a shelf full of books and shoved it at her. "Your homework."

Kara opened the book and flipped through it. Each page depicted a rune, with notes on its uses below. There were hundreds of them. The runes called to her, beckoning her to touch them. She snapped the book closed and tucked it under her arm.

"Pick out some runes you're interested in. Memorize them. Practice drawing them—*not in blood*, unless you want to lose a finger. We'll start from there."

Salizar held out an empty vial and a small knife. "Now, my sample. Are you comfortable doing it, or should I?"

Kara took the knife and vial. It might be more in character for Lady Grey to ask for help, but she didn't want Salizar carving on her with a knife. She made a small cut through the middle of her mark, suppressing a shudder as a wave of sensation wracked her. She slid the vial against her skin, collecting the blood, then capped it.

Salizar's eyes were greedy as he took the vial from her and tucked it into the pocket of his robes.

"When should I return? For my lessons."

"I'll send for you."

()

KARA HID the vial of demon's drip in the back of one of her vanity's drawers, tucking it beneath a velvet pillow cushioning a pearl necklace. The vanity was full of expensive jewelry like it. If things went sideways and she had to escape the capital in a hurry, she could make a tidy fortune fencing them. She put the leather pouch of syringes in the bottom of the armoire, beneath the heavy skirts of her dresses. She needed a better place to hide things from Merry, but the floor and walls of her chamber were all stone—she'd have to chisel out a hiding place if she wanted one.

Kara crawled into bed with the grimoire, closing the curtain around her, and propped herself up on the pillows. The book creaked as she opened it and braced it on her thighs. She thumbed through the pages, looking through different rune names and their designs. Kara stopped when she came to a page titled 'Sound.' There were several rune variants depicted on it. One could hold a message that'd play when someone activated the rune with blood. Another variation allowed eavesdropping by pairing a rune at the location she wanted to spy on with a mirror rune attached to some token or object.

An adjustment to the eavesdrop rune had been sketched in the margins of the grimoire in ink. Beneath the sketch, it read, *'Mirror rune may store messages for later listening.'* Kara grinned and bent the ear of that page. That one would prove useful.

Her eyes drifted down the page. Another note in the margins read, '*May be runed onto the skin beneath your ear for a direct sound link. Wouldn't recommend. High propensity for madness.*'

On the page for 'Sight,' there were similar runes, allowing someone to record images of a location or open a peephole portal into the location they'd like to spy on. '*You can see them, but they can see you, too! Useful on ceilings.*'

The implications of such spells were staggering. Salizar could know everything that was happening in the castle if he wanted to. If he had the library runed, he may already know her true identity. Was he toying with her?

Kara continued reading, flipping deeper into the book.

Unlock / Lock

Unlock a locked door or chest, or prevent entry except to those whose blood makes up the rune.
Ineffective on someone's secrets.

Pain

Drawn on the body, will cause pain varying in intensity according to size of rune.
Merge with fire rune to cause burns.

Passion

Draw on the two targets you'd like to feel impassioned for one another. Beware, passion quickly becomes rage.
Do not mistake passion for love.

Health

Helps heal a wound or combat an illness. Only effective on minor wounds and illnesses.

As Kara got farther into the book, she wondered who it had belonged to. Marginalia riddled the pages—someone had spent a lot of time on these notes and rune customizations. But Salizar didn't seem like the type to lend out his personal grimoire. She flipped to the front again, looking for a name or initials, but there were none.

The runes in the latter half of the book grew complicated, the instructions and list of precautions longer and more dire. Some runes had to be paired with incantations or performed during a specific phase of the moon. Simple rune shapes became several runes knit together to form a larger rune. One design spanned two pages.

Transport

Place an object on a blood-charged rune to transport it to the rune's mirror.

Teleportation possible in theory, but so far people have only managed to teleport pieces of themselves.

Shield

Creates a hardened blood shield around the area the rune is drawn on. May be drawn on skin.

Search

Track an item or person.

Can be used to search a room for the presence of other runes or spells.

Sacrifice

Someone had ripped everything below the title of the sacrifice page out of the book. Kara found the sanguinata rune in the last few pages. She'd begun to doubt she'd find it. It read, '*Blood binding. Bind your blood with another's. Can be used to influence someone's thoughts, heal them from a gravely injured state, or form a link that can't be broken.*' The description was frustratingly vague, and there were no helpful notes in the margins. Kara wanted to know how long the effects lasted —and what did 'a link that can't be broken' even mean?

Kara closed the book, retrieved a piece of paper and quill and ink from the drawer of her bedside table, and practiced the runes for eavesdropping and unlocking. She repeated that until she'd committed them to memory, then burned the pages in the hearth and stuffed the grimoire beneath her mattress.

CHAPTER FOUR

Kara missed Logan. She wanted his advice, his warmth, his strength. The safety she felt when he was around. The palace was lonely, for all the people in it, and she wasn't making much headway with her mission. The people at court were cliquish, not swift to accept an outsider. And aside from her Stygian clan members, she'd never had much luck befriending people.

Her keening was getting closer every day, and she needed to figure out a plan before it was too late. Logan had said he'd be back within the month, but she was nervous. She could try Salizar's antidote, but what would Logan do? Find someone who needed killing? Be with someone else? Her mind rebelled at the idea of him with anyone but her. She wished she'd pressed him harder for answers before he left.

Kara glanced at the armoire containing the lover's bowl when she returned from a ride around the palace grounds, temptation warring inside her. She ought to be charming courtiers and finding information for King Calim before he fired her, but she'd been horribly distracted lately, both by Logan and her late hours spent memorizing blood runes.

The bowl taunted her with its possibilities. Maybe she could find out where Logan was, how far away. Kara cursed and withdrew it from the armoire.

She filled the bowl with warm water and sat down with it on the floor of the bathing chamber. Her hands shook as she lowered it to the ground, sloshing water over the edge. Who else did she have a strong enough bond with to scry for? Would she be able to see where Wesley had gone, answer once and for all if he'd returned to the Sanguines? Kara gazed into the water and brought to mind a memory from their childhood, when Wesley had defended her from a group of children chanting 'Kara the Cursed has a demon nurse.' Wesley had pummeled the boy leading the chant to the ground, earning a black eye in the process. He'd been her champion when they were little, but over time she'd become his burden. An obligation he resented.

The water swirled, and Kara's heart jumped into her throat. Then it went black and faded slowly until the water returned to clear. She sighed. It'd been a long shot, she supposed.

Kara focused on the water again and thought of Logan. An image bubbled to the bowl's surface, becoming visible as the water settled.

Logan was in a tent, the flap closed. *Argh.* She wouldn't be able to tell where he was.

He reclined on a pallet, head resting against his saddle, flipping some tattered piece of paper over in his hands. Caressing it like a talisman. She wished she could tell what he was thinking. He looked much the same as before, though his beard had grown in more and he had dark circles under his eyes.

The tent flap opened, and the woman from the last

time Kara had scried entered. Kara's stomach tightened into a knot. The woman wore diaphanous pants suited to an arid environment and a cropped dark blue top embroidered with crystal stars that bared her midriff. Logan sat up and folded the tattered paper he'd been holding, stuffing it into his pocket. He made to rise, but the woman knelt beside his pallet, stopping him. She laid her hand on Logan's, and Kara's grip on the edges of the bowl tightened. *Damnit, Vakarian. Do something.* They spoke back and forth for a moment, their words unintelligible. Kara had always been terrible at reading lips.

Then the woman leaned in close and pressed her lips to Logan's. Her hand drifted to his chest, and she moved to straddle him. Logan didn't move, didn't pull away. Didn't do anything. An eternity passed in a second. Kara saw red. The outer edges of the bowl crumbled to dust beneath her fingers, and the image swirled, turning black. Her mark lit up with a fiery red glow. Rage burned in her belly. A glance in the mirror confirmed her irises were a vivid red. It took everything in her not to slam the bowl against the tile and shatter it into a thousand tiny pieces, pulverize it until it was unrecognizable. She stood up from the floor, hands coiled tight into fists, her entire body tense as emotion sawed through her chest. She wanted to run out of the palace until there was no one in sight, so she could scream at the sky.

( )

KARA SLEPT LIKE SHIT. She tossed and turned in her bed all night, got up periodically to pace in front of the fire until she was falling asleep on her feet, then crawled back into bed again. After seeing the kiss, she'd gone to the training yard to drill for hours, exercising through her tears. When the sun set, she came inside to drill some more, pushing her body to its limits until all she could think about was the next pushup, the next punch, the next breath.

It hadn't been enough. What a fool she'd been to believe in him. To fall for him.

A quick rap on her door woke her, and Kara slid her eyes open into slits. Judging by the sun coming through the window, it wasn't even noon yet. She planned to spend the entire day—nay, week—in bed, crying and resisting doing bodily harm to others. Punctuated by an irresponsible amount of drinking.

"What?" Kara groaned.

Merry swept into the room, beaming. She carried a silver platter that held a steaming cup of coffee and a thick invitation card.

"What's that?"

"An invitation."

"So?" What the bloody hell was she so chipper about?

"It has Lord Kendrick's seal," Merry squealed.

Kara winced at the sound.

"Are you not pleased, my lady? Viscount Kendrick is— well, he's everyone's ideal man."

Kara snorted and grabbed the card.

"Are you alright, mistress? Your face is very red this morning. You look a might peaky."

"I'm fine." Kara ran a nail under the card's the thick wax seal, breaking it, and unfolded the note.

Lady Grey,

I have today off, if you'd like that tour of the city you requested. Meet me in the stable yard.

Yours,
Aidan

KARA ROLLED her eyes at '*Yours, Aidan.*' She was loathe to go. The man had disastrous timing.

Merry read the note over her shoulder, then squealed and shuffled her feet. "What would you like to wear, mistress?"

"Who said I was going?"

"You—you're not?"

The level of censure in her voice made Kara blink. She dropped her head into her hands and rubbed her temples. Kendrick was the best connection she'd made at the palace besides Serena and a mage that wanted to bleed her. It'd be foolish to miss this opportunity. She couldn't let Logan disrupt her life anymore than he already had. If anything, her contract with Calim was even more important now.

Kara collapsed backwards into bed. "Whatever you deem suitable, Merry. I've no energy for decisions today."

Merry's eyes lit up. She hustled to the armoire, pulled out a low-cut, golden dress the modiste had sent, and laid it out on the bed. "We must do something with your hair, my lady."

"Must we?"

A week ago Merry would have probably apologized for being too presumptuous, but she was growing used to Kara's attitude. She nodded fervently and patted the back of the dressing chair.

Kara rolled out of bed, slow as a sleepworm, and plopped down in front of the vanity. She motioned blindly for the coffee, and Merry passed it to her.

Merry began to brush Kara's hair out, and Kara closed

her eyes and relaxed into the sensation. "Are you good with hair?"

"I have four younger sisters that I practiced on."

"You'll have to remind me when mine looks a mess. In the country there was rarely a need."

Fifteen minutes later, Merry had braided and wrapped Kara's hair into an artful arrangement that hid a score of pins. Kara fought the urge to scratch her scalp.

Merry slid open one of the vanity drawers, and Kara's heart stuttered, hoping it wasn't the one with the demon's drip. She relaxed when Mary pulled out a necklace and a pair of earrings strung with yellow crystals. The shade matched the dress perfectly.

Merry passed her the earrings, and Kara paused when she realized the implication. Her ears weren't pierced. She'd had no jewelry growing up. Why put a hole in a perfectly good earlobe?

"My ears aren't pierced."

Merry looked more taken aback than when Kara had stripped in front of her. "Really? Most women in Lerathil have their ears pierced as children."

Kara shrugged. "Never got around to it."

"I can do it for you, if you'd like. I did my sisters'. With proper care, the risk of infection is low."

The offer surprised Kara. It'd be a small sacrifice to fit in at court, and in truth, she thought piercings looked dashing on both men and women. "I'll take you up on that."

Merry put the earrings back and draped the necklace around Kara's neck, snapping the clasp closed with a click.

Kara hardly recognized herself in the mirror. Seeing herself like this made her miss a part of herself that'd never existed—made her imagine a life where her parents had survived the Curse Wars and she'd had a normal childhood. She had no memory of her parent's faces; she'd been too young. As a child, she'd convinced herself Da was her real father, ignoring Wesley's insistence on disabusing her of that notion.

"Would you care for any cosmetics? Glamours?"

Kara tilted her head back and blinked away a tear. Of course the aristocrats were rubbing magic on their faces. "Not today, Merry. Thank you. This is perfect."

"You don't need them. You look beautiful. Kendrick will fall at your feet."

AIDAN WAS LEANING against a sleek black carriage in the stable yard, looking every inch the noble. A team of two dappled greys was already hitched, and he smiled as Kara approached. "You made it."

"Wouldn't miss it for the world," she said between gritted teeth.

He held open the carriage door for her and took her hand, helping her inside. Kara slid into the plush seat. The interior of the carriage was warm, and black velvet curtains framed the windows.

Aidan climbed inside and took the seat opposite Kara. The carriage was large by most standards, but his tall frame filled the space. Knees clad in buckskin breeches brushed against Kara's as he settled in his seat.

Kara was used to traveling on horseback in the open air. The carriage felt like a cage, a barrier between the wealthy and the world they lived in. "Where are we headed?"

"First stop, the water clock. You likely saw it on your way into town, but it's a marvel up close. It's what Lerathil's known for, besides the palace of seven spires."

He rapped on the carriage roof, and they rolled into motion, heading for the gate.

Kara peered out the window as two guards opened the tall palace gates, revealing a bustling city just down the hill. One tower near the center loomed higher than all the other buildings. The carriage jolted forward as the driver cracked the reins, and their knees knocked together.

"You seem distracted today. Did something happen?"

Kara turned to Aidan. "I'm sorry. I received some disappointing news last night, and I've yet to compose myself."

"Ah. So that's why you were stabbing sandbags in the training yard for hours. Dare I ask who you were imagining?"

Kara raised an eyebrow and sat up straighter. "Are you having me watched, Lord Kendrick?"

Aidan smiled, but it didn't reach his eyes. "I'm simply doing my job."

"And since when did it entail keeping such close tabs on me?"

"My offices overlook the training yard. Useful for keeping an eye on lazy recruits. Though while we're on the topic, I heard you went to visit Salizar. Did he do something to upset you? I've never liked the man."

"Well. Your future wife won't keep any secrets from you, will she?"

"Are you petitioning for the job?"

Kara forced a smile. She wished she had a fan to help hide her expressions and combat the blasted heat of this carriage. "I wouldn't need to petition."

Aidan blushed and glanced at his knees, still touching hers. "My apologies, Celine. I shouldn't be treating you like you're under investigation. I've had eyes on Salizar's chambers recently."

"Is there cause for concern? I sought him out for a simple herbal remedy for a headache."

"Nothing concrete. Just general unease, really. It's likely nothing." Aidan shifted in his seat and pointed out the window. "You can see the water clock from here."

A wooden tower rose amid the buildings packed into the heart of the city. It was a cross between a water mill and a clock tower. Troughs scooped water from a pool at the tower's base, carrying it up to a wide clock face. As the troughs tilted over, water funneled out of the clock's mouth, resulting in a continuous waterfall. Intricate metal gears and cogs, exposed by breaks in the woodwork, turned within, powering the mechanism.

The carriage pulled to a stop behind the crowd gathered in front of the tower, and Kara and Aidan exited.

"Would you like to go to the top?"

Kara looked over the mass of people gathered in front of the pool, splashing their fingers in the water and tossing wish-laden coins in. "That's allowed?"

"There's stairway access for when repairs are needed. It's not accessible to the public, but they'll let me through."

"One of the benefits of being captain?"

"Indeed." Aidan grabbed her hand and led her around the back of the tower. After a brief exchange with two guards stationed in front of the door, they were let in. The din of the crowd faded as they climbed the rickety wooden staircase. The rush of water and steady creak of cogs made Kara feel like she was climbing through the belly of a great machine beast.

The stairs peaked at the top of the tower, behind the clock's face. The sun lit the clock with a pale glow, and the troughs emptied load after load of water into a metal chute that tilted forward once it was full, creating the waterfall.

"This is amazing."

"I find it peaceful, despite all the noise."

Kara held out her fingers as one of the troughs emptied, letting the water run over her hand and catching a stray coin.

"Tell me about yourself, Celine. You're something of an enigma at court. All I know about you is that you fight."

"You don't find enigma appealing?"

"Maybe for a fortnight."

Kara chuckled. "A straightforward man, then."

"It's why I went for the captaincy—no head for politics. I'll leave that to my father and brothers."

"What do your brothers do?" *Besides torment their peers.*

"It'd be faster to tell you what they *don't*. I've four of them."

Kara smiled. "Humor me."

"One's running the estate with father, one captains a ship in the eastern sea, one joined the mother's temple, and the youngest, goddess help him, joined a mercenary clan."

Kara bit back her smile. "You disapprove?"

"The clans are the reason the crown is struggling. Urian gave them too much power during the Curse Wars."

Kara decided to nudge him. "Who did he join? The Sanguines? I hear they're the largest."

"The bleeders of the people? No, thank the mother. He was curious about them—I'm glad he didn't end up there. They would've been a bad influence. He's already the unlikeable sort. He joined the Stygians. The people's shadow."

"I know what you mean. My brother—" Kara clamped her lips shut as she realized what she'd said. She'd let the eldest Kendrick son ease her off her guard. She had to be more vigilant, regardless of what was going on with Logan. He'd lured her up here out of sight, and she hadn't even brought any weapons with her.

"You've a sibling? I didn't know the earl had one child, let alone two. Are they a bastard?"

Kara's heart thudded in her chest. "Not my actual brother, sorry. A childhood friend—as good as, since I grew up largely in solitude."

Aidan furrowed his brow, but he didn't push the issue. "Speaking of siblings, we received news that the princess is near. Calim's masque will be held soon."

"How exciting."

"Will you save me a dance?"

"Of course. Though I'll imagine you'll have a busy night. I've seen the girls in the training yard."

Aidan tugged at his collar. "They look at me like a piece of meat. You, however…"

Kara leaned against a wooden column by the clock face, each splash of water sending a light spray of droplets toward her. "How do I look at you?"

Aidan propped a hand over her head and leaned in towards her. "Like an equal." His other hand traced her jaw, and Kara spotted the intention in his eyes. She ducked under his arm and spun around him before he could lean in for a kiss, flashing him a brilliant smile. "This must be the spot you bring all the girls. Very smooth."

Aidan broke into a deep laugh. "We should go before the guards come searching for us."

Kara fell asleep soon after they returned to the carriage, lulled by the rocking and steady shuffle of the horses' hooves. She woke with a start as the carriage hit a rough patch of ground. She wiped drool from the corner of her mouth, and Aidan laughed.

"I'm sorry. It's not a reflection on your company. I didn't sleep well last night."

"Not to worry. I appreciate a woman who knows how

to relax. I'd hoped to show you some other spots in the city, but we can do it another day."

Kara "Thank you for the lovely distraction." She'd been able to keep her mind off Logan most of the day.

"My pleasure, Lady Grey."

CHAPTER FIVE

Kendrick's information about the princess's return proved true, as next week the invitations for the masque went out. Salazar had yet to invite Kara back to his workshop, but she'd been studying the runes every night before she slept. It was slow-going, tedious work. Her hearth was laden with ash from all the practice pages she'd burnt, but some of the runes were intricate and needed to be drawn from start to finish without stopping.

She'd taken up Merry on her offer to pierce her ears for her. The maid had done it with a hot needle and a cork pressed behind her ear, swift and decisive. The pain had been minimal, and she'd healed quickly. Kara quite liked the look of the king's jewels dangling from her earlobes, catching the light. Merry had even convinced Kara to practice walking in heels in preparation for the masquerade. Kara was convinced they were demon shoes better suited as weapons than footwear, but she practiced nonetheless.

She was beginning to feel the slow encroach of her keening, like a shadow at the edge of her vision. She was considering taking the demon's drip once it began in earnest. *Or perhaps you can take a lover on the side of your own.* There'd been no word from Logan still, and the evidence in the bowl had been damning. Perhaps someone at tonight's fête would interest her. Kendrick might be game, but he seemed to be looking for something more serious than a fling. And while they had a friendly camaraderie, Kara felt no real connection with him. No spark. Nothing like the hyper-awareness she felt around Logan Vakarian. Damn that man.

On the evening of the ball, Kara had Merry come to her room early to help her get ready. She'd already scrubbed and clipped and shaved within an inch of her life. Kara would be wearing her favorite gown from the modiste—a sleeveless black and crimson number that plunged between her breasts in a deep vee. The fabric wrapped around her breasts and navel, curving into sharp, thorn-like points. It was the loveliest thing Kara had ever worn.

"Lace me tighter tonight," Kara said as Merry helped her into her corset. She was pulling out all the stops—she needed to drop jaws and disarm people. She'd strapped one of her jeweled daggers to her thigh beneath her shift, in case she ran into any trouble. There'd be lots of unfamiliar faces at the party.

Kara had put a rush order on a mask from the modiste that matched the dress, but it hadn't arrived until earlier today. Kara slid lid off the mask box, and her mouth fell open. The mask was large—delicate red lace surrounded the eyeholes, and raven feathers were intricately layered beneath the lace, arching down over the cheeks and sweeping back over the forehead. Two large black horns curved out from the mask's temples, rising into vertical points. Only her eyes, lips, and jaw would be visible beneath it. She didn't know what the modiste charged for this—the bill went straight to Calim—but it was a work of art.

Merry peered over Kara's shoulder. "You wanted to be a demon?"

Kara smiled at the irony. "I didn't specify. I just asked that it match the gown."

"It's striking. Most of the women wear simple lace and feather masks or half masks, so their faces are still visible."

"I don't care. I love it."

Merry nodded. "People will remember it."

Kara decided to wear her hair down beneath the mask, and Merry curled it with a pair of metal tongs she heated in the fire. Kara had planned to wear an entire set of ruby and onyx jewelry, but with a mask this lavish, she didn't need it. She opted for a pair of ruby drop pendant earrings instead.

She moved to her window and gazed out. From her room, she could see carriages lining up at the entrance of the palace, one after another on a path bordered by statues of past Telerian leaders. Fae lanterns floated between the statues, casting a rainbow of colors across the procession. The line extended past the gate and wrapped around the street. Anyone who could talk—or pay—their way into an invitation would be here tonight.

Merry called her back to the vanity and painted Kara's lips wine red and lined her eyes with dark kohl. Kara slipped on a pair of black heels, then sat so Merry could tie the mask behind her head and clip the edges into her hair to ensure it didn't fall.

Kara preened in the mirror when they were finished. The kohl liner made her eyes pop behind the mask, and she felt giddy with power. She was beautiful, otherworldly —a demoness destined to make men kneel. She was also incredibly uncomfortable. Her toes were already scrunching against the sides of the shoes, and her corset was tighter than she was used to. The mask's large horns added extra weight to her head, which was likely to give her a headache if the night went long. And everything was so tight, it'd be a challenge to get to her dagger with any speed.

"How long is this ball again?"

Merry laughed.

◯

Two glasses of wine into the ball, Kara was enjoying herself immensely. A group of magical creatures paraded past her, dancing and laughing. Foxes and rabbits mingled with fauns and minotaurs, their eyes bright beneath their masks. A man in a dragon mask pulled a giggling fairy into a curtained alcove. The masks, the dresses, the music—*this* was what she'd expected when she'd dreamed of Lerathil, when she'd seen its sprawling spires and sparkling night sky —not empty corridors and cryptic mages to a humble king.

Where had all these people been for the last month? Did they hole up in their manor houses for winter and return with spring? Or was the princess the true life of this city? Princess Ariana had yet to make an appearance— fashionably late, Kara supposed. Or perhaps she was here in secret, disguised beneath a mask to enjoy her chance at anonymity. Now that she thought of it, the man in the fox mask she'd danced with earlier had a frame similar to Calim's.

Kara flitted between groups of guests, never intro- ducing herself as she hung on the corners of their clusters like decoration. She eavesdropped on their conversations, listening for hints of displeasure with the king and any gossip that might prove valuable.

Whilst prowling the ballroom for leads, she'd been looking for anyone who caught her fancy, someone she might want to keen with. When she felt guilt or hesitation, she summoned the image of the stranger kissing Logan in the bowl and held that rage high in her chest. She'd failed with Vhaidra, but that felt like an eternity ago. She was determined to proposition someone tonight, when the mask would hide her true feelings. The demon's drip lingered at the back of her mind like a dark promise. Kara shuddered, the thought of plunging it into her skin covering her exposed flesh in goosebumps. She could do this.

Kara had already danced with several men, all forgettable, but the second half of the evening featured dance cards for the new debutantes—a convenient way to arrange introductions to potential suitors. Her name was among the cards. She'd promised a dance to Kendrick, but she'd yet to identify him in the crowd.

It was difficult to choose with everyone's faces hidden, but a tall man by the drink carts had caught her eye. He was broad-shouldered, with a muscular build beneath his black breeches and doublet. His dark hair was pulled into a knot at the nape of his tan, muscular neck. Many of the courtiers here grew thick from their desk work and the rich foods they could afford, unless they enjoyed some sport or vice, but this man obviously stayed active.

The stranger turned as his companion, a tall man in a royal blue coat with the mask of a golden lion, approached with a drink. The movement exposed his face. He wore the mask of a snarling black wolf, its fangs exposed. All that was visible of his face were thin lips and a chiseled jaw shadowed by a short beard. Kara quite liked the look of him. If he proved not to be insufferable, perhaps she'd ask him. She definitely hadn't seen him at the palace before; she would have remembered.

Kara made her way over to the table the dance cards were laid out on, eager to inspect hers and investigate who'd made the list. She frowned when she pulled hers out of the pile. A single name was written into every slot. *Lord Melbourne.* She cursed. How was she supposed to meet potential suitors and ply them for information when some selfish fuck wanted to monopolize her evening? She was going to have a word with this 'Lord Melbourne.' Kara didn't recognize his name, but there were a lot of new people here this evening.

She glared at the servant attending the dance card table and slid her card in front of him. "Who let this happen? You?"

He bit his lip and dropped his eyes. "He—he paid me good money for it. I've got a new child at home, my lady. I needed the coin."

Anger beat behind her eyes, encouraging her to flay him with her words. Kara took a deep breath. She couldn't blame the man. She knew what it was like to be desperate.

"I'm sorry, my lady. You don't have to dance with him at all, of course, if you don't wish to. Do you want a new card?"

It was too late for that; the dances were due to begin any minute. Kara shook her head. "Point me to this Lord Melbourne."

Kara followed the shaky finger the man raised. He pointed to the man in the wolf's mask.

Kara blew a hard breath through her teeth. *Of course.* She moved to the wall next to the drink carts, setting up where she could keep the wolf in her sights. She'd make him come to her. The man filling drinks kept staring at her breasts and over-filling the glasses. She'd never worn a dress so low-cut before, but she was willing to put up with the leering if it got her information. Plus, it made her feel sexy and powerful.

The masque's officiator climbed to the top of the ballroom's staired entrance and announced that the dance card portion of the evening had begun.

The wolf immediately turned, locking eyes with her. Like he'd been aware of her location the whole time. He began striding toward her, his dark eyes sliding over her skin. She failed to suppress the thrill that ran down her spine.

Kara turned away from him and scanned the crowd, avoiding his gaze, but she felt his presence as soon as he arrived.

"Masquerading as a wallflower?" the wolf asked. His voice was deep, with a smooth accent, but Kara couldn't place it.

"It seems I'm out of options, since some unfeeling cad thought to monopolize my dance card."

"You wound me, Lady Grey."

"An unrepentant cad, too?"

"You are the only woman here I wish to dance with."

"Then your night will be short." Kara rose her hand in front of his face and released the fist she'd been clenching, letting the tiny, torn up pieces of her dance card sprinkle to the floor between them.

The grin he flashed her was utterly wicked. "Oh, I beg to differ."

Kara smiled despite herself. "You're very confident, but it wouldn't be fair to my other prospects for me to dance with you alone."

"I don't give a damn about the others. I've made my intentions clear."

"Come, Melbourne, we've just met. Such commitment is a rarity among lords. Are you ready to propose as well?"

"If you'll have me." Then he was down on one knee, pulling something out of his pocket.

Kara snapped her eyes to him. Surely he wasn't—

And then she saw what he held. A dance card, *Celine Grey* scrawled at the top in a strong, masculine script, and below that, a single instance of his name. *Lord Melbourne.* The other revelers were beginning to turn and stare.

"One dance. That's all it will take."

Kara laughed, unable to hold it in. "You're persistent."

"You have no idea."

Kara flushed straight down to her core. This man was unnerving her. "And yet you can't even convince me to dance."

Melbourne rose from his knees and stepped closer, his height making him tower over her. "I believe you'll dance with me."

She tilted her head back and looked up at him. His eyes were dark behind the mask, pulling her in, and he smelled like the *sun.* They stood indecently close; there would be gossip about them tonight. "What makes you so certain?"

"I could feel your gaze on me across the ballroom before we ever met. You want me."

Kara stilled. Their verbal sparring was making her blood run hot, and she was undeniably attracted to him. He would make a fine candidate for her keening. She ran her tongue over her lips. The strains of a waltz were beginning in the background. "One dance."

Kara offered him her hand, and he took it in his gloved one and pulled her toward him. He escorted her towards the dance floor, his hand on the small of her back.

He led her into the dance with confident, graceful

steps, keeping his dark eyes trained on hers. Kara relaxed and let him take the lead. His hands were warm, and his long fingers engulfed her palm in his.

Melbourne's gaze danced over her face. "You're the most beautiful demon I've ever seen," he said, his voice rumbling.

"Have you seen many, then?"

"In the mirror."

"And here I thought you a hungry wolf."

"For you, I am ravenous."

His muscles bunched beneath his doublet as he spun her around and lifted her in time with the music. His strength was alluring. The touch of his hands on her waist and shoulders was lingering, possessive. Kara liked the feeling of his hands on her.

"How long are you to be in Lerathil, Lord Melbourne?"

"For a time. Depending on my impetus to stay. I heard you were husband hunting."

"The rumors are true, I'm afraid."

"And what qualities do you seek in a husband?" Melbourne purred.

Kara thought for a moment. "A partner. Trustworthiness. Someone willing to share the entirety of themselves with me, and I with them."

"I'm jealous already."

They made a swift turn to avoid bumping into another couple, and Kara winced at the pinch in her toes.

"What's wrong?"

"My feet hurt. I made poor choices in footwear."

"We could take a turn around the garden, and you could take your shoes off. And whatever else you'd like."

"Trying to get me alone?"

"Of course." Melbourne winked behind his mask, and Kara's heart flopped over in her chest.

She was strangely tempted to take him up on his offer. "There is something I'd like to ask you."

"Anything."

Kara took a deep breath, steeling her will. She conjured to mind the image from the bowl. "I've been told that it's not uncommon for marked women to ask the men at court to help them with their keening. Mine approaches."

The wolf went still, faltering in his steps for the first time that night. His lips wrinkled with displeasure, and his hands tightened on her.

Was he upset that she was marked? Perhaps she shouldn't have told him. She could've taken him to bed without declaring the fact.

"So I've heard," he said, his voice tight.

"I'm in want of a…companion."

"And are those qualities you seek in a husband the same you'd like of your *companion*, Lady Grey?" His eyes hardened on her, no longer the soft, enraptured expression of a moment ago, and his voice bit.

Kara considered her answer, then shook her head. She didn't want Melbourne to think she was looking for a long-time partner. "I'd need discretion. Flexibility. Impermanence."

"Are you waiting for someone, then?" He studied her eyes with his, searching for something. The waltz was lulling down, the dance almost over. Their spinning had led them to the center of the dance floor, midst the swarms of other couples.

"No." *Not anymore.*

Melbourne yanked her closer to him until her body pressed against his. He was all steel. He lowered his head to hers and pulled her hair aside to whisper into her ear, his breath tickling her neck.

A shiver swept Kara's body, and she quivered in his arms.

"In that case—" His voice shifted, the accent falling off, "Are you asking for me to fuck you, *Kara?*"

The blood froze in Kara's veins. Her heart started to clamor in her chest, alarms sounding in her head. He knew her. She'd been found out. Who was he? She reached up and ripped the wolf's mask off by the snout.

Logan Vakarian stared down at her, a cruel smile on his lips.

Kara stumbled away from him, stunned. *"Logan?"* she whispered. He was tanned and bearded, his hair grown out, but it was undeniably him. She was a fool.

His mask fell from her fingers. Several people around them turned to look on, tittering behind their masks.

Heat coursed up her cheeks. Of course it was him. Who else would inspire that kind of reaction in her? She hated him in that moment. For tricking her, for lying. For putting on that fake accent. How dare he be angry. The urge to leap into his arms and kiss him warred with the desire to slap the malicious smile off his face. The latter won. Her hand hit him with a crack. Her palm stung from the force of it. He could have stopped her; he saw it coming. He let it happen—didn't even flinch. A red mark in the shape of her hand bloomed on his cheek. His beautiful, sun-kissed cheek. Kara wanted to make him bleed. She'd have to do it with her words.

"In answer to your question, *Melbourne. Anyone but you.*"

His eyes went amber, and his hands clenched into fists at his sides.

A trumpet played from the large stairwell that spilled into the northern end of the room. The princess had arrived. Kara stepped backward into the crowd of bodies surrounding them. Logan reached out to grab her, but he, for once in his godsdamned life, was too slow.

The crowd compressed as people moved, en masse, towards the stairs to await the princess. Kara began shoving people out of her way, muttering, "Excuse me, pardon me."

The officiator cleared his throat, and the music died. "I'm honored to announce the return of our beloved Princess Ariana to Lerathil, the city of stars." The crowd began to clap.

Kara glanced back. Logan was moving towards her, but he was getting trapped behind the crowd. He couldn't barrel through them without injuring someone and making even more of a scene. People shoved at Kara, trying to get closer for a better look at the princess. She was hot inside her mask. There were too many people, too much noise. She was trapped. She had to get out of here. She kicked off her heels, leaving them in the middle of the crowd.

Dimly, outside the buzz and rage of her thoughts, she heard the officiator say, "We have the Stygian Brotherhood to thank for her safe return."

Kara stilled and slowly turned towards the stairs.

A petite woman in a sprawling midnight blue gown descended the steps. Her ash blonde hair fell in a curtain down her back, and a translucent veil trailed the ground behind her. She twinkled when she moved. Small diamonds had been sewn into the fabric of her dress and veil, and a sparkling silver diadem crowned her head. She was captivating, iridescent. If Kara was the night sky, she was the stars.

She was...familiar. Then the man in front of Kara stepped to the side, and she got her first good look at the princess's face. She wore a half-mask fashioned to resemble a swan's wing, leaving the other half of her face bare. It was the woman from the lover's bowl. The woman who'd kissed *her man* and moved to straddle his hips.

Kara's nails bit into the palms of her hands, drawing blood. *The princess? The fucking princess she was supposed to be protecting?* Claws raked through her soul. She was going to kill him.

The princess reached the bottom of the stairs and continued to move forward. The crowd parted like the sea in front of her. Kara caught Logan's eyes with her own. He stared at her with naked intensity before turning away. Ariana came to a stop in front of Logan, and Kara's stomach sank like a rock.

Logan bowed low for the princess, then took the thin-boned wrist she offered and kissed her white-gloved fingers. Kara was unraveling. She couldn't watch anymore; she wanted to vomit. She wished she had her shoes back. Logan wasn't here for her.

She resumed pushing her way through the wedge of humanity, heading towards one of the servant's entrances at the side of the room. She needed to get out of here. If the Brotherhood had escorted the princess here, there'd be Stygians all over the palace. She flashed back to the moment she'd first spotted Logan and the man in the lion's mask. *Jon?* Their builds were similar. Did they know she was here? Would she run into Thomas lurking in the dark hallways, looking for revenge? It was clear she no longer had Logan's protection.

Kara made her way back to her rooms, anger seething in her breast. The evening was ruined. She'd discovered no information for the king, and Aidan would be disappointed she hadn't danced with him. The dancing would continue late into the night, but Kara couldn't trust herself to return in this state. She'd be liable to blow her cover. Gossip about her slapping 'Lord Melbourne' would already be spreading like wildfire, and she'd be expected to explain herself.

She slammed her door behind her and yanked her mask out of her hair, wincing when the clips ripped several hairs free with them. She began struggling in vain to yank the tight dress off her body.

"Need a hand?" someone asked.

Kara whirled. Jon lay on top of her bed, tossing an apple she'd left uneaten earlier in his hands. His clothes confirmed his identity as the golden lion from the ball. He looked much the same, bright eyes and gleaming copper hair, though he'd also grown a tan.

"*Jon.*" It felt like a lifetime since she'd seen him last. It'd been before her reckless prison break for Wesley. Emotion swelled in her chest, and tears threatened.

"Wanna trade rooms?"

He was joking with her, just as he'd always done. He wasn't angry or accusing; he was just *Jon*. Tears spilled over her cheeks.

Jon rolled out of the bed and strode over to her. "Why the tears? I'm an expert at undressing women. Though you do look ravishing. I told you red was your color."

Kara gave him a half-hearted shove, and he pulled her in for a tight hug. "Missed you, Ace."

He smelled so good—clean and fresh and masculine. The castle always smelled of dust and incense. He cradled the back of her head in one hand and lightly massaged it.

"You don't hate me?" she said against his chest.

"Hate you? After prison break like that? I'll never let Logan live down getting himself drugged."

Kara pulled away from him. "Be serious, Jon."

"I don't hold it against you, Kara. When Logan told us

the prisoner was your brother, I understood. I would have done the same for mine. I just wish you'd trusted us enough to tell us."

"I thought you were an only child?"

"He died when we were young. I'm here for you, okay? Whatever you need."

"I need to get out of this dress." Kara twisted around, motioning toward the flat line of buttons hidden beneath a flap of fabric.

Jon quickly undid the majority of the buttons, his expression in the mirror tight. When he neared her waist, he stopped. "That should be sufficient," he said in a hoarse voice.

Kara shrugged out of the dress, letting it pool around her feet.

"God's teeth, woman. I'm not made of stone."

Kara glanced down at herself. The tightly laced corset was pushing up her breasts, and the lace border of her black stockings was visible beneath the thin slip. "You offered."

"I didn't dream that you'd take me up on it."

Kara chuckled. "I need help with the corset." It occurred to Kara that Jon might be willing to help her with her keening. He was attractive, and he made it obvious he liked her—though Kara never considered it anything more than a close friendship before. She didn't want to cause strife between him and Logan, though. They had enough bloody history together.

Jon shuddered. He loosened the laces at a speed to rival Merry, keeping his gaze trained on the corner of the room. "Off with you, before I do something we'll both regret."

Kara rose an eyebrow at him and sat down at her vanity, where she began to pull pins out of her hair and remove her jewelry and makeup.

"Are you planning to stay in Lerathil?"

Jon took a seat on the patterned chaise lounge under the window and scrubbed a hand over his face. "Yes. Another contract. The King wants a lot of eyes and muscle on this."

"Who all is here?"

"Everyone from Travincal. We rode directly for the Karashae desert, once money for the escort was in hand and we were through—" Jon paused. "Through hunting you. Rohan will have turned Raven's Rest on its head by the time we return. The horses may be living in the great hall as we speak."

"Thomas?"

"In the musician's booth tonight. He's not bad at the triangle. Faedra and Aaron were waiters."

"I need to speak with him. Apologize."

Jon shrugged. "If you wish. You taught him a valuable lesson."

Kara scoffed. "Not to trust anyone?"

"Not to let his guard down in situations like that, even to a friendly face. If you'd been a Sanguine spy, he'd no longer be in possession of his guts."

"And what of *Lord Melbourne*?"

"An actual title, awarded by the king himself. The court knows he's the Stygian Commander, but he's still accepted here. He's a curiosity for them."

"You're telling me that King Calim hired someone called Lerathil's Bane to escort his sister across Teleria *and* gave him a title?" Had the title came with any lands? Did Logan have an entirely different life waiting for him outside of the clan, but chose the clan anyway?

"How do you think Calim became *King* Calim? Troublesome councilmen and political detractors can live a long time if left to their own devices."

Apparently Logan's disguise at the ball hadn't *all* been a ruse meant to trick her, but it still rankled. "What happened in the desert, Jon? With Logan and the princess?" Would he tell her the truth of it?

Jon rubbed the back of his neck. "I...I don't know. She's the flirtatious sort, was after him like a dog with a bone. I think it was a sticking point for her that he didn't immediately succumb. She's bent out of shape about her betrothal and looking to rebel."

"Did anything happen?"

"I sincerely doubt it, Kara. The man's crazy about you. He set a devilish pace across the Karashae, determined to get back here before the month was out. And it's not a hospitable climate, to say the least."

"It doesn't matter. He's too late."

"You've...keened already?"

Kara glanced away from him. Let them believe what they wanted. She rose from the chair, propped her leg up on it, and slid her dagger from its sheathe on her inner thigh. It was the only place to hide a weapon when she wore form-fitting gowns, and she had a small bruise where the pommel had rubbed against her skin.

Jon made a strangled noise in his throat. "So that's where you've been keeping those. I'm sore you never thanked me, by the way."

Kara stilled, swinging her eyes to his. "They were from you?" She'd half-thought Logan had been lying about not getting them for her this whole time.

"Who else?"

Who else, indeed? "How extravagant," Kara said, crossing the room to him on bare feet. She held his gaze with hers. His throat bobbed as she neared, eyes darkening. "Excessive." She ran her finger under his jaw and tilted his face up to hers. "And lovely."

And then Kara kissed him. She didn't know what she was thinking. She was drunk on power, drunk on his lust for her. She wanted something to fill the gaping hole in her chest. She wanted to destroy.

Jon's hands clenched the edge of the couch when her lips touched his. He was still at first, unresponsive. Kara's demon roared. She lowered herself into his lap and wrapped her hands around his neck. His muscles went taut beneath her. A silent war waged within his body.

Then his hands dove into her hair, and his lips awoke beneath hers, kissing her back. His kiss was slow and sensual, explorative. He nipped at her lips, coaxing them open for his tongue. Where Logan's kisses were a streak of flame straight to her loins, Jon's was a slow burn. A steady blaze to Logan's wildfire.

Jon pulled away, his expression heady. "We shouldn't do this."

"Was that thank you enough?"

The sound of splintering wood echoed through the room.

Kara jerked her head up. Logan stood in the doorway, eyes ringed red, pieces of the broken door frame clenched in his fists. Rage pulsed off him in waves.

"Logan—" Jon started.

"Don't, *second*." His voice was dark, furious. A muscle ticked in his jaw, and he twisted his neck, stretching it out. Then he closed his eyes and whispered under his breath.

Was he…counting?

Logan's shoulders bunched, every muscle in his body shuddering. Then he turned around and strode away. A few seconds later, a loud thud came down the hallway.

Kara stared at the shattered doorframe in shock. It was made of thick, solid pieces of timber. She rose off of Jon's lap on shaky knees, and he stood up behind her.

"Fuck. This is not good. In fact, it's very, very bad."

"Are you going to talk to him?"

"Mother Night, no. I'd like to keep my head attached to my body. I'm amazed he was able to walk away." Jon ran both hands through his hair, gripping the ends in his fists. "I don't know what I was thinking."

"You shouldn't feel guilty. It's nothing he hasn't done."

"What are you talking about?"

"I saw him kiss Ariana."

"How—you know what, I don't want to know. Did you kiss me just to get back at him?"

Kara looked at her feet and drug a toe across the floor. "I was caught up in the moment, but I'd be lying if I said that wasn't a factor."

Jon groaned. "You'll be the death of me, woman."

The memory of the scar spanning Jon's back, put there by Logan the first time he'd awoken and lost control, filled her mind. "I'm sorry." Her eyes brimmed with tears, the events of the evening starting to catch up to her.

Jon tilted her head up and put his hands on her shoulders. "Kara McKenna, I love everything about you except that you're not mine. But Logan is my best friend. So if you ever choose me—" Jon's voice hitched, and Kara's heart ached for him. "I want it to be because you want me, and only me. Not because I'm your second choice."

"I love you, too, Jon, but—" *Not like she loved Logan.* Her breath halted at the admission she'd made to herself. If only they were different people, in a different life.

"I know." Jon closed his eyes and drew in a deep breath, then a smile slowly spread across his face. As if he hadn't just spilled his heart onto the floor. As if she hadn't just crushed it. He was an expert at donning the mask.

"I wish it were you. I feel awful about this."

"Cheer up. Stay strong. It will all work out, okay? Now, I'm going to go hide until he calms down."

Kara laughed through her tears. She walked Jon to her door, pausing when she saw what sat on the other side of the shattered frame. The black heels she'd abandoned during the masque rested outside her door, perfectly aligned.

CHAPTER SIX

Merry shrieked when she entered Kara's room, dropping the tray of coffee she carried. The cup shattered against the marble floor, and the dark liquid began seeping into a large puddle.

Kara jerked up in bed, eyes wild. "What is it? What's going on?"

"You—your door! What happened?"

Kara blinked, turning her head to glance at the mangled doorframe. Shit. "I, um—I leaned against it, and some pieces broke off. The wood must have been rotten for a while." It was far from the most convincing lie she'd ever told, but she had no rational way of explaining it. *My Namirahn lover shattered it with his bare hands because he saw me kissing his best friend.*

Merry edged around the spreading pool of coffee and pulled open the curtains, letting a burst of sun in.

Kara squinted as the harsh light hit her eyes. "I really wish you wouldn't do that."

"You should rise, my lady. A royal hunt has been announced."

"Calim didn't strike me as the bloodthirsty sort."

"The *King* does not hunt. The princess has arranged it."

"Oh. Of course she did." Because a riding party full of of armed people, including the princess and Logan, was exactly what she needed right now. "How bad would it look if I skipped out, Merry? I'm not feeling well today." *I've only managed to ruin most of my relationships in the last twenty-four hours.*

Merry frowned, the skin between her eyebrows tightening into a little wrinkle. "It's the princess's first outing since her return ball. Everyone who's anyone will be there." Merry eyed Kara with a knowing look. "You're flushed. Were you up into the wee hours of the morning? I expected you to ring for help undressing last night."

"I...managed."

Merry smirked. "I'm sure you did. You don't have to actually hunt, if you don't wish. Many of the ladies ride in the back, gossiping and flirting."

Kara nodded "I'll go." She needed to make up for her lost opportunities at the ball, while everyone from outside the city was still at the palace.

She dressed in tan breeches, a form-fitting white blouse with a high collar, and brown leather riding boots. Kara'd seen few women in Lerathil riding sidesaddle, and breeches didn't seem a far cry from the split riding skirts the Vespertines wore. She equipped her weapons belt with her jeweled daggers, grateful for an opportunity to wear them exposed. Merry helped her braid her hair into a tight plait that started at the top of her skull and fell to the middle of her back.

On her way to the stables, Kara discovered the victim of Logan's rage last night. He'd punched a large hole into the wooden wall a few doors down from Kara's room.

Blood smeared the wood. Kara winced and continued towards the stables.

THE HUNT WAS to take place in the king's private forest behind the palace. The hunting party gathered in the stable yard, most of them already mounted when Kara arrived. Based on the number of plumed hats in attendance, she was decidedly underdressed.

"Lady Grey," the stablemaster said, bowing to her. "I've readied your mount."

"Thank you." The man led her to the tall grey mare with black stockings she'd been riding during her time at the palace. She let him help boost her into the saddle. She could easily mount without assistance, but appearances needed to be maintained.

Several large black hounds clamored around the riding party, eager for the chase. Serena and Aidan were present and mounted. There was no sign of Jon, unsurprisingly. When Kara spotted Logan's broad form atop Char, a pang went through her. She could almost pretend they were back in Raven's Rest, heading out for a training exercise. Logan cut a handsome figure in his tan breeches and long black riding coat. She liked seeing him in clothes other than Stygian leather—she could almost pretend they led normal lives. His bone bow was strung across his back, his quiver full of arrows fletched with raven feathers. He didn't turn to look at her once. The pit in Kara's belly grew.

Kara glanced at the other members of the riding party. She recoiled when she saw Princess Ariana exiting the stable leading Drum. Jealousy flared up Kara's spine. Why was the princess of godsdamned Teleria riding *her* horse? *Still.*

Kara cut her head to Logan, catching him looking at

her. She shot him a look that could curdle blood. He raised an eyebrow.

Ariana swung into the saddle with no assistance and trotted up to them. Kara watched her like a hawk, looking for signs of poor horsemanship. If the princess donned a crop, Kara was prepared to give her hell.

The princess's eyes swooped over Kara, assessing her in a glance. "Lady Grey, I presume? I don't believe we've met before."

Kara bowed her head. "The pleasure is mine, your highness."

Ariana's flinty stare swept away. "Let's head out," she called. The riders shifted in their saddles and began heading for the distant tree line. "Ride with me, Lady Grey."

Kara pulled her horse even with Drum at the front of the party. Logan fell in on Ariana's right, with Serena and the other Vespertines forming a larger ring around her and the party as a whole. Was he her bodyguard now? Or something more?

"You're quite the mystery at court. No one seems to know anything about you. Last night's bit of business proved entertaining, though."

"I had too much to drink, I'm afraid."

"He probably deserved it."

Kara wished she could disappear, just ooze from the saddle and melt into the earth.

"I've heard you're on the hunt for a spouse." Ariana gestured to two women who rode at their flank. Kara had seen them around the palace and the training yard, though they hadn't been introduced. "Pippa and Tanith, my ladies-in-waiting. They're nuptially-keen as well. Though I wouldn't get in their way if I were you."

Pippa wore glasses, and her brown skin contrasted

beautifully with her violet dress. Tanith reminded Kara of a cherub. Short auburn curls danced around her round face, and she had striking grey eyes.

Kara nodded at them. "Lovely to meet you. I'm Celine."

Drum kept pulling at her bit, moving her head towards Kara. "Where did you come by your beautiful mare, princess?"

"She's Lord Melbourne's. A marvelous animal. I rode him—I mean her—frequently on our way back from Karashae City, when the carriage became too stuffy. I'm tempted to buy her off of him."

Kara bristled at her slip of words, rage hot behind her eyes. Was she baiting her because of what had happened at the ball? Or did she suspect her true identity? "Is she for sale, Melbourne?" Kara asked, unable to keep the bite from her voice. She would never forgive him if he sold her.

"Not my horse to sell."

"Ah, yes. Not his horse, supposedly, though he brought her to the desert. So I asked among his mercenaries about her owner, yet none would tell me *whom* she belonged to."

"What are we hunting?" Pippa asked.

"Deer, boar, whatever we come across." Ariana turned around and raised her voice for the rest of the party. "There's rumored to be a white stag with a sixty point rack in these woods. I'll reward anyone who takes him down handsomely. And whoever claims the best kill today shall sit at my side at the feast tonight!"

The party cheered. Kara's eyes slid to Logan's bow.

"I should like to see that white stag," Kara said.

"You doubt it exists?" Ariana asked.

"Every hamlet in Teleria has its fabled white stag, golden goose, or sleeping dragon. More likely a cow escaped someone's fence, or a bored hunter had a bit too much to drink."

"Well, you may hunt the normal deer if you wish. Though I see you've no bow. Do you know how to shoot?"

Kara shook her head. "Poorly," she lied.

"Pity."

"May I take my leave, Princess?" They were nearing the forest, and Kara didn't want to be at the front of the hunt's mad dash.

Ariana agreed with a wave of her hand and turned to talk to Logan.

Kara slowed her horse and drifted to the back of the party, where Aidan fell in by her side.

"I missed you at the ball last night. Was that you, the demoness?"

"Unfortunately."

Aidan's lips twisted. "What happened?"

"Lord Melbourne was a bit too forward for my liking. I took offense."

"Be careful with that one. He's mercenary scum."

Kara stifled her frown. His derision grated. "I had to leave after the altercation—I was too embarrassed to stay."

"Well, you didn't miss much. Some lambs humping satyrs in the alcoves, one belligerent crow too deep in his cups."

Kara chuckled. "What did you attend as? I didn't spot you in the crowd."

"An eagle."

"Suits you."

A hound bayed in the distance, alerting the party to the scent it'd found. The horses' ears flickered, and they danced in place. The hunt master blew his horn, and they were off, the hunters of the group charging into the forest.

The party's sedate tail wandered apart, sprinkling out

around the lake at the forest's edge. Young lovers glad to be rid of their chaperones wandered into the shadowy parts of the forest, and those too old and bloated to hunt mopped sweat off their faces and adjusted their belts. She and Aidan were alone.

An older matron named Lady Sheridan was coaching her team of servants through unfolding a blanket and setting out glassware far too fine for the outdoors. "I've prepared a picnic while we wait for the blood sport to be finished," she called. "Do join us."

Aidan gestured to the picnickers. "Shall we?"

"Why not?" Sitting next to Lady Sheridan was Lord Rutherford, a man of some influence at court that she'd been meaning to introduce herself to.

They made their way over to the group and dismounted, leaving the horses free to graze.

Aidan introduced her, and Kara knelt atop the blanket they'd laid out on the grass. Lord Rutherford was a plump man with a thick mustache and wire glasses. He didn't strike Kara as the traitorous sort, but the most successful traitors wouldn't.

Rutherford pulled a dark bottle out of a wicker picnic basket. "I've brought a bottle of my estate's best whiskey to share."

"Oh, goddess, I remember the trouble last time we got into this stuff," Lady Sheridan said.

"Trouble?" Rutherford said. "You mean pleasure, raucous pleasure."

Lady Sheridan blushed and glanced away. They were both married to other people, but that didn't mean much in Lerathil.

Kara hid her smile and held out her glass to be filled. She took a sip and coughed, caught off guard by the harsh taste. It slid down her throat, settling into a warm glow in her stomach.

Aidan turned down the whiskey and began cutting an apple into thick slices, occasionally lifting the blade to his mouth to eat one.

Rutherford set his bottle down and lit a pipe. A smoky vanilla aroma filled the air.

Aidan offered Kara a slice of apple, and she bit it out of his hands without thinking.

"How is your husband hunt coming?" Lady Sheridan asked, staring pointedly at Aidan. She had all the subtlety of an elephant.

"I hope this hunt will be more successful," Kara said, gesturing towards the forest.

Rutherford glanced between her and Aidan. "You two'd make a fine couple. Where are you from again, girl?" He pulled on the pipe and blew the smoke into the middle of their group.

"Briarcliff. Lord Grey is my father."

Rutherford sputtered. "Well. I'll have to ask him about that one at our next game of cards. You don't have the look of his get. He always did have a weakness for the wenches, though. Hmph. His late wife is probably twitching in her grave."

Kara gulped and took another sip of whiskey. Hopefully Calim's leverage over the Earl was sturdy enough to secure his silence. "And your estate, Lord Rutherford? Where do you hail from?"

"I've a house in the city, but my ancestral seat is in the Black Hills. That's where we make the whiskey."

She raised her glass. "It's divine."

The Black Hills were Sanguine territory. He'd be a ripe target for an alliance, or even blackmail. Did the Sanguines have something over him? "Lord Kendrick and I were discussing the clans the other day. Do you have any trouble with the Sanguines at your estate?"

Aidan stiffened beside her, and Lady Sheridan snapped her fan open and began rapidly fanning herself.

"No, actually. They're perfectly civil. I'd be more concerned about that Stygian whispering in the princess's ear."

"You mean Lord Melbourne?"

"Lord? Please. Another of Calim's shortsighted gestures. He's a degenerate. A dog in black leather. Why he's welcome at court at all is beyond me. Mercenaries and royals shouldn't mix. I wouldn't trust him on the hunt, in the dark of that cursed forest. Too many nobles go missing when that one's around."

"Now, now, Ruthy. Calm down. You know I hate talking politics over lunch."

It had occurred to Kara that Logan may be the one hired to kill Ariana. Was that why he'd let her kiss him? But whose money would he be willing to accept for that kind of job? Not the Sanguine's. Who else would want the princess dead? Kara stole several more apple slices off Aidan's plate. He smirked and began peeling another one.

Lady Sheridan took a long drag from her whiskey glass. "I'm surprised you learned Melbourne's true identity so quickly, Celine. Was that the source of your altercation last night?"

"Something like that," Kara murmured into her glass.

"Have you met him before?" Sheridan asked. Kara knew her sort. Like a dog with a bone or a small, squeaky animal. Determined to flog the question until they'd squeezed out every bit of juice. She'd have to give her something to get her to heel.

"No. My maid shared some of the kitchen gossip surrounding his arrival with me, that's all. He, ah—he thought to monopolize my dance card last night. I took umbrage."

"Good stuff always happens when I'm at the card tables," Rutherford muttered. "Still, he's a bad influence on Ariana. Can't have her going the way of Calim. So eager to right the sins of his grandfather he can't see what's right in front of him."

Lady Sheridan swatted at Rutherford with her fan. Aidan asked him a question about the whiskey-making process, which set him off on a mind-numbingly detailed explanation.

Kara stared into the treeline. Even the birds avoided the royal forest, choosing to perch on the few trees scattered across the open field rather than land in that lush tangle of branches. All she'd managed to learn was that Rutherford hated Logan and wasn't shy about his dislike for Calim's politics, but it was a start.

By the time she finished her second glass of whiskey, Kara's bladder caught up with her. She excused herself and walked into the forest, where the shadows pressed in on her, crowded and thick. She'd expected something groomed over and cleared out, with well-delineated paths, but it was much more primitive than that. The forest whispered under its breath. Unintelligible voices tickled her ear, just out of reach.

Kara walked farther into the forest for privacy, then leaned against a tree and pressed her forehead into the bark, letting its ragged edges abrade her skin. Light stretched through the trees in staccato bursts. It was a relief to be alone, to have a moment to be herself. Keeping up the appearance of Lady Grey was a welcome distraction from her issues with Logan, but the entire charade was wearing on her spirit. A reckoning between them was coming, and she wasn't sure she could weather the storm.

Kara squatted in a nearby bush and relieved her bladder. A shadow moved at the edge of her vision as she pulled up her pants. She whirled around. No one was there.

She was jumping at shadows. She'd drunk too much whiskey too quickly, and it was clouding her senses.

Kara glanced down to buckle her belt.

Then her shadow moved, but Kara *didn't*. Icy hands wrapped around her throat, squeezing tightly. She tried to tuck her chin, but it was too late. Who the fuck had managed to sneak up on her? Kara gripped the hands choking her, clawing at them with her fingernails, and pain shot across her hands. As if she'd been scratched…

She stepped to the side and swept her legs beneath her assailants', bringing them both to the ground. Kara blinked as her attacker rolled away, not fully comprehending what she was seeing. A being made of shadow rose from a roll to its feet in a smooth, practiced motion. It was transparent, the forest murky but visible through its body. It had the curves and bust of a woman. Was it some forest spirit she'd stumbled upon? Why the hell was it so angry?

The shadow launched itself at Kara, eating up the ground between them with long strides. Kara barely scrambled to her feet in time, her reactions sluggish. She blocked the shadow's punch and kicked it in the gut. White hot pain seared her abdomen. She stumbled backwards at the same time as the shadow creature. It felt like she'd been kicked by a horse.

Kara regained her footing and studied the creature closely as it circled her. The shadow woman was favoring her left side, where Kara's own abdomen ached. Kara blocked the creature's attacks, staying on the defensive and studying her attack patterns. It was the same way Kara fought, with quick, darting bursts and lithe dodges. When Kara glanced behind herself at where her shadow should be, her fears were confirmed. There was nothing there.

How was she supposed to fight her own shadow when every strike she scored hurt herself? Thank the goddess she hadn't tried to stab it. She could hardly kill it. Was this a spell? Had something at the picnic been spiked? Rutherford had consumed the same things as everyone else.

Kara hesitated to call for help. There was no telling who from the hunting party or picnic might show up, and they'd have questions she couldn't answer. But she had an idea. Magic separated her from her shadow, but magic tended to follow the path of least resistance.

Kara began leading her shadow deeper into the woods, where the tree canopy knit together and less and less sun broke through. It began to flicker at the edges, its legs slipping flat against the earth, then rebounding into its full form as it staggered towards her. The shadow was becoming difficult to see, but light still spilled in from the edges of the forest. Kara backed into a tree, then spun around it. The shadow leaked towards her still, growing large and thin. Fear pulsed in her chest. Darkness, she needed darkness.

She turned and ran, looking for an escape. The trees closed in around her, reaching for her. Kara slid to a stop next to a small ravine. Dead leaves and bracken filled it. She scrambled down the steep incline and dove into the mulch, scooping up sodden leaves and earth and goddess knows what, burying her face and limbs until no light leaked through. Her heartbeat pounded in her ears. Minutes passed. A whooshing wail filled the ravine, and icy fingertips gripped Kara's jaw, prying open her mouth. Her shadow fed its frigid fingers into her mouth, her nostrils. Kara tried to grapple with it, and her hands met cold smoke. She struggled to swallow, to breathe. Ice plugged her airways. Then the presence atop her vanished, evaporating into tiny ice crystals that settled atop her body. Shadow smoke fled down her throat, and Kara drew in great, gasping breaths, desperate for air.

She sat up slowly and moved a hand into the light. Her shadow danced across the edges of the ravine, following her as it ought to rather than trying to choke her out. Kara collapsed back into the mulch, resting a moment and catching her breath. The ice crystals scattered across her clothes were melting, leaving her damp and chill.

Emotion bubbled up in her throat as her heart ceased trying to escape her chest. The tidal wave she'd become so accustomed to holding back overflowed, and she started to sob. Great, wracking sobs that left her short of breath. Tears flooded her cheeks. She cradled her head between her knees and let it take her.

She cursed Logan and Wesley and Calim and this forest and this fucking contract. Cursed Da for ever plucking her out of the muck to begin with. She let go of the months of frustration and pain that she kept such a tight rein on. Having to don a mask all the time meant she never had time to relax and be herself. Combined with losing Logan and her own shadow trying to kill her, it was too much.

Aidan's voice filtered through the trees, still distant. "Celine?"

Kara scrubbed her dirty hands over her eyes and forced several deep breaths into her lungs, willing herself to calm.

Aidan rounded the corner on his horse, his eyes widening when he saw her. He swung out of his saddle and slid down the ravine toward her. "Celine. What's wrong? Are you hurt?"

Kara tried to compose herself, drawing tight on Celine's puppet cords. She was still shaken. "Just my pride and a rolled ankle, I'm afraid. I got turned around on my way out of the forest and slipped down here." Let him think her the damsel in distress. She wasn't far from it at the moment.

"Why didn't you call for help?"

"I did. No one heard me. Thank the goddess you came this way."

"Blasted forest. I'm glad I found you. The hunt's over, everyone's heading back to the castle. You would have been alone out here."

Already? How much time had passed? Kara shivered and crossed her arms, tucking her fingers into her armpits. No one around to find her body or hear her screams, had her shadow been successful.

Aidan pulled off his hunting jacket and draped it around her shoulders. It was toasty warm and smelled of expensive cologne.

He squatted beside her, his muscles stretching beneath his shirt. "You're sure you just rolled it? Do you need me to check if it's broken?"

Kara shook her head. "Rest and some ice will set me to rights."

"Good," he beamed at her. "Wouldn't want my new favorite sparring partner to be out of commission."

Kara gave him a genuine smile, and he wrapped his arms beneath her armpits and helped her to her feet.

She favored her left ankle and leaned into him as they stood.

"Can you make it up the ravine? It's too steep for me to carry you."

Kara nodded, and they clambered up the steep slope together, Aidan keeping a steady arm around her back. At the top of the incline, he lifted her up onto his horse, then mounted behind her.

"Why'd you come after me?" Had he unleashed the shadow spell and come to finish her off? She hated to believe it of him, as kind-hearted as he seemed, but she couldn't trust anyone.

"When you were gone for so long, I grew worried. It's easy to get lost in these woods. The groundskeeper used to cut them back, but every time they grew back with a vengeance, even larger and more wild than before."

"They are rather unsettling."

"The forest is Namirah's creation, you know. It was flatland before, but she missed the woods she played in in her youth, so she grew it from a few saplings into this monster."

"It's just been twisted from its true nature." Likely a side effect of the dark magic of the curse tainting the ground.

Aidan paused, then nodded. "You're right. But next time you venture here, make sure you're not alone. This forest is hungry."

"Are you disappointed you didn't get to join the hunt? I'm afraid I diverted too much of your time."

"I care little for the tradition. The dogs chasing the prey, the bloodthirsty nobles racing for the kill. I come because it's expected of me, but I prefer nature to the slaughter."

They reached the edge of the picnic clearing, but Kara's mount was nowhere in sight. "Where's the mare I rode?"

Aidan's chest brushed against her as he twisted in the saddle. "That's odd. I hitched her here when I left. Maybe the others took her with them?"

Kara's suspicions rose. First the shadow attack, now

this. Someone was trying to kill her, which meant her identity was compromised. She replayed the events of the afternoon in her head, committing everyone's faces to memory. The perpetrator might have been among their group, and it could be the very person plotting against Ariana—or someone connected to them.

The hunting party was mid way back to the palace by the time she and Aidan caught up with them. A large brown buck was draped over Char's hindquarters, and one of the arrows from Logan's quiver was missing.

Kara ignored the jealousy daggering at her insides. Apparently he wanted to be near the princess at dinner, too. Maybe he was helping to guard Ariana now, but it still stung.

Curious faces glanced at her and Aidan riding together, turning to whisper once they'd spotted them. Kara didn't see her grey mare among the party.

Logan turned ever so slightly in his saddle, his eyes cutting across her face, then Aidan's. His expression tightened. Hope swelled inside her that he might still care, but she shoved it down into the pit of her belly, where it could roil amongst the whiskey and other thoughts she shouldn't have.

Logan said nothing. Kara relaxed against Aidan's chest and closed her eyes, hoping she caused Logan a fraction of the pain he did her.

"Will you be attending the feast tonight?" Aidan whispered into her hair.

It was the last thing she wanted to do, but she was on the king's dime, and regaining her place with the Stygians was seeming less and less likely. Plus, she needed to ask Serena about the shadow creature—could it come back and try to strangle her in her sleep? She checked the ground for her shadow and saw it blurred with Aidan's.

"I'll be there."

( )

KARA TOOK a long bath and dressed for the feast in another of the modiste's form-fitting, low-cut numbers. When she arrived at the great hall, a servant in blue livery stepped forward to escort her to her seat.

Kara did a double-take when she looked at the servant. "Faedra?"

Faedra winked. "Hullo again. You look a picture."

"Care to trade places?"

"I'm not in for all that posh stuff. Me and Aaron been conspiring below-stairs, trying to convince this lot to strike."

"Talk to Merry. She deserves a raise."

Faedra's smile twisted. "Quite the stunt you pulled, back West."

They neared the head of the table, and Kara slowed her steps. "I know—I'm sorry—"

"Ain't me you need to apologize to. Thomas wants you to meet him in the belfry at midnight tomorrow."

Kara bit her lip. The perfect place for an ambush. Dark, removed from the palace proper. Few people to hear her scream. "I'll see what I can do."

They drew to a stop by the long dining table. "Don't worry, I got you the best seat in the house." Faedra gestured to a chair directly across the table from Logan Vakarian.

Kara swallowed the rock in her throat and took a seat. "Lord Melbourne."

His eyes slid through her like she was a feature of the terrain. Rage swelled in her chest. She wished she could unleash it and breathe flame. She could handle his hate, but his indifference was so much worse.

Princess Ariana floated into the chair beside Logan, and cold prickles ran across Kara's skin.

Serena sat down at her right, and Kara released a breath. "Thank the mother you're here."

"I don't miss venison nights."

A parade of food was ferried to the table, more than they'd ever manage to eat. The venison was roasted to a golden gleam and flavored with apples and honey. Mounds of glazed bread braided into different shapes and platters of cheese and fruit crowded the table. One of the servants put a thin slice of meat onto her plate. Kara drained the wine from her goblet and raised the empty glass. A servant hurried to refill it.

Logan was calm and collected in his conversations with the table. He showed no signs of being perturbed, as if he hadn't crumbled timber with his rage last night. She hoped Jon was still breathing.

Serena glanced between her and Logan. "There seems to be some tension in the air," she whispered to Kara.

Kara snorted. "Do you know of a spell that would make one's shadow attack them?"

Serena's eyebrows rose. "Why do you ask?"

"Mine tried to strangle me in the forest earlier. During the hunt."

Had Logan's jaw twitched at that?

Serena frowned. "Shit. Are you okay?"

"I'm here, aren't I?"

"Grouchy tonight, I see." Serena popped a grape into her mouth. "Such spells exist, but they'd need a piece of you, a strand of hair or something, to perform it."

"Or blood?"

"That would work."

Kara grit her teeth. She was overdue for a talk with Salizar. "Is there a way to determine who cast it?"

Serena speared a piece of venison with her knife, brought it to her mouth, and chewed. "We can try. Come to my workshop later."

As dinner progressed, Kara had trouble keeping her gaze off Logan. The glow of the candelabras lit the indentation at the base of his neck. She wanted to lick that groove of tanned skin. Kara shook her head as a familiar heat curled between her thighs. Stupid fucking curse. Her keening approached. Soon the dreams would begin, the flushed, sensitive skin and naked longing.

Ariana used any excuse she could to touch Logan. She whispered things in his ear, touched his arm to ask him to pass a platter, gripped his shoulder when she laughed at something he said. Logan took it all in stride, even smiling and joining in on her jokes with Pippa and Tanith. He was sickeningly charming.

Kara took another long sip of wine. She'd rather be flayed than sit here and watch this. Her mark pulsed insistently beneath her cuff, hungry.

"Oh, Commander," Ariana said, tilting her beautiful head back in a laugh. Everything about her was exquisite. Kara pictured blood dribbling down the princess's throat, staining that pale flesh. Her fingers curled around the handle of the cutting knife beside her plate. Her food was still untouched, her belly full of fire.

Serena laid a hand on Kara's thigh and squeezed, then leaned in toward her ear. "Calm. Your eyes are glowing."

Kara jerked up from the table, her chair scraping against the floor in a harsh whine. Everyone seated around them stopped talking and stared at her.

"Leaving so soon?" the princess asked.

"I've had enough. I was stuffed full earlier today."

A flicker of orange lit Logan's eyes, and she bared her teeth in the semblance of a smile. She'd made him crack.

Kara hurried out of the great hall, eyes heavy on her back. She stumbled back to her chambers, leaning against the palace walls when she lost her balance. She'd drunk far more than she'd eaten today, and it was catching up to her.

She hated him. Hated the princess. Hated this dress and her doomed mission.

She crashed into her rooms and grabbed one of her daggers, then slid it through her stays, cutting through the corset and dress. She didn't want to be around anyone right now, not even Merry. They could take the dress out of her pay if they wanted. She needed to talk to Logan, hash things out between them. She was going to jeopardize her contract with Calim if they let this go on any longer.

Kara crawled into bed and stared at the ceiling. She wished he'd show up at her rooms, all anger and passion. She'd make him explain what she'd seen in the bowl, like she should have done to begin with instead of kissing Jon. She imagined them arguing and it devolving into passion-ate, heated sex. He'd look at her with molten intensity, and she'd melt for him. She grew slick at the thought.

Kara thrashed on the bed, kicking her legs at the mattress. Would she even be thinking these things if not for Namirah's curse? She hated its control over her, that she was beholden to it every month. Her eyes drifted to the drawer in the vanity where the demon's drip rested.

She tried to sleep and failed. Images from this evening and the scenes from the lover's bowl plagued her mind. Her mark pulsed against her cuff, heating the silver until it was burning her skin. Kara ripped it off and threw it across the room.

Would Logan be in Ariana's bed tonight? Could he even say no to the princess of the realm? After sweating into the sheets and pulling one corner free with her thrashing, Kara relented and rolled out of bed. She rubbed the rune on the fae lantern by the vanity, filling the room with a blue glow. The fire had died down to embers.

Kara retrieved the syringes from the armoire and fished the vial of demon's drip out of the drawer. She eyed the potion suspiciously. Was there more of it than there'd been before? She shook her head. It'd probably just spread out when it'd rolled around the drawer.

This wasn't an ideal time to suppress her strength, but she couldn't handle this dance along the knife's edge of lust and anger without help. At Raven's Rest, she'd turned to drink. That wasn't an option here. Something had to give, and taking her keening out of the equation was a good start. And then she'd know once and for all how much of her attraction to Logan was a byproduct of the curse.

Kara unstoppered the vial and inserted the needle into it, then sucked up the potion. She expected it to be difficult to draw up the thick liquid, but it crawled almost eagerly into the syringe. Salizar had stoppered shadow.

Kara looked over the veins on her hands and arms, then reconsidered. She'd do it somewhere less visible, in case her skin reacted to it. She pulled off her slip and eyed the vein in the hollow between her navel and hip. It would do. She took a deep breath and slid the needle beneath her skin. It was relatively painless. Some of the tension in her shoulders faded, and she began pushing in the plunger.

Nothing happened at first. Then ice gripped her veins. Bitter cold raced along her skin, and Kara grit her teeth. She forced herself to finish pushing in the potion. Her hand shook as she pulled the needle free.

Thin black tendrils began to spread beneath her pale skin, branching out from the injection site. What the hell was happening? Salizar hadn't mentioned this. The tendrils moved quickly, twisting and curling towards her navel. Then they abruptly stopped. Kara let go of a shaky breath. She'd been afraid they were going to travel across her whole body, marking her flesh. Hopefully it wasn't permanent.

Pain staggered her, blossoming in the pit of her belly. Kara bit her tongue to keep from crying out. It was like the worst menstrual cramp she'd ever experienced, magnified by a hundred, and it felt *cold*. Her mark flared a bright orange color, then slowly dimmed, fading until the mark was just a scar on her wrist, as it'd been before she'd awakened. *Must be working.* The fading of the familiar glow unnerved her—like she'd snuffed out some vital part of herself.

Kara stumbled towards the bed and crumpled to her knees when another wave of pain wracked her. Claws raked the inside of her skin, struggling to get out. She drew her knees up to her chest, curled into a tight ball, and rocked back and forth until the pain started to subside. She crawled the rest of the way to the bed, pulled herself into it, and collapsed.

CHAPTER SEVEN

Merry arrived at her usual time in the morning, which was way too fucking early.

Kara screwed her eyes shut against the light stabbing at her eyes when Merry threw open the curtains. Merry knelt to gather the dress from last night and cursed when she saw the torn fabric. It was the first time Kara had heard her swear using anything other than 'trickle biscuits.'

"My lady…"

"I know, Merry. I had far too much to drink last night."

"Lately your room looks as if you turn into a beast once the sun goes down!"

Kara chuckled, then winced as the movement sent pain shooting through her head. Her body was a collection of dull aches. Is this what normal people felt like in the morning?

Merry sat the coffee tray on the small table beside the vanity. Her eyes fell on the empty vial and syringe Kara had left out last night.

Fuck. Kara was getting way too sloppy. She was naked

beneath the covers, black veins all over her belly, and the silver cuff that hid Namirah's mark was still wherever she'd tossed it last night.

Merry turned to look at Kara, her lips twisting into a tight frown.

"It's a tonic I take. For health. When I was a child I was quite sickly, so I still take medicine to ward off illness."

Indecision flickered in Merry's eyes, then she returned to tidying the vanity. "And ye've got to stab yourself with it? You poor thing. Makes me shiver just to think of it."

If only you knew.

"Shall I pick out a dress for you to wear today?"

"Is the princess throwing another surprise event?"

"Not that I know of."

"I'll be wearing pants, then. I'm going to have a bath first, though. Thank you for your help."

Merry finished tidying the room and left. Kara hoped she kept her lips sealed about her mistress's *anomalies*.

Kara dragged herself out of bed and went to the bathroom, locking the door behind her. She gasped when she saw her reflection in the mirror. A black, twisting sunburst arced its way across her left hip and abdomen, dark as ink. The scoop of her navel was a disconcerting purple color. Had the marks spread further overnight?

From here out she'd have to don her undergarments before Merry arrived to dress her, so she didn't see it. Kara began running her bath, trying not to think about how she'd traded one mark for another.

Kara finished dressing and sought out Serena in her workshop, eager to see if she could trace the origin of the shadow spell. The spire's endless stairs had her slightly out of breath, when usually she would've been able to jog up them. She glanced at her abdomen and sighed. She'd have to take things easy for a while as she adjusted to the side effects of the demon's drip.

Serena was bent over her workbench, hammering at a silver sword. She turned when she saw Kara enter and wiped sweat away from her brow.

"Kara." She frowned and crossed the room to Kara, dark eyes quizzical. "Your aura's different. Did something happen?"

Kara smoothed her expression and shrugged. "Could it be an effect of the shadow spell?" She had no intention of telling her she was taking Salizar's antidote. The less people who knew she was in a weakened state, the better.

Serena's lips curled into a frown. "Maybe. I expected you last night."

"I needed to calm down after the feast. Plus I was drunk."

"Vakarian driving a woman to drink? Never."

Kara grinned. "So, how does this spell tracing work?"

Serena nodded at an arcane circle chalked onto the stone floor. "Stand in the middle. Face the window so your shadow stretches behind you."

Kara moved to the point. Serena stood in front of her and traced her fingers across Kara's forehead in the shape of a rune. A strange energy began buzzing across Kara's skin, like a million butterflies flapping their wings.

"Are the runes used in blood magic the same as the ones you use?"

"Some of them. But for blood magic, the catalyst is the power in your blood. Mages like me draw their power from the earth and environment." Serena floated her hands down Kara's body, holding them a few inches away from her skin. Warm yellow energy lit the gaps between her fingertips.

Kara sighed in contentment. Serena's magic tended to have a relaxing effect on her.

"Have you gone to Salizar, then?"

"Yes. He hasn't shown me anything yet, though."

Serena's magic hummed, and Kara's shadow began to split. A second shadow stepped away from it. It was only a silhouette, its shape jagged at the edges. Someone thin, and the silhouette's shape suggested they were wearing a dress. The silhouette shrank away to nothing. Serena cursed.

Kara frowned. "A woman?"

"The energy signature is feminine, but I couldn't tell much beyond that. It's faint. You should have come to me last night."

Kara grimaced. "I've had a lot going on."

Serena threw up her hands. "More important than someone trying to murder you?"

Well, when she put it like that... "Should I worry about my shadow trying to attack me in my sleep?"

Serena shook her head. "The spell's negated for now. They'd have to cast it again, for which they'd need another piece of you."

"Can Merry be trusted? I never thought my hairbrush could be used against me." She'd have to start burning the hair regularly, but it'd be impossible to find it all, as much as she shed.

"This is Lerathil. No one can be trusted. But something like a hair or nail, already dead, would provide a weak connection. How strong was this shadow?"

"Very. It felt like I was fighting a copy of myself."

"Then it's more likely they fueled it with blood, saliva, something like that."

Kara really needed to pay Salizar a visit. She bit her lip. "Someone must know my identity."

Serena nodded. "We'll keep you undercover for now, but stay wary. It's likely they'll try again."

()

Kara pounded on Salizar's door, her nose curling at the acrid stench that crept beneath it.

He swung it open, expression tight, relaxing a little when he saw her. "Lady Grey? You knock like a soldier."

"My urgency is only exceeded by my concern."

"I'm glad you're here, actually. I have some rather unfortunate news—"

Kara crossed her arms and arched a brow at him. "Yes?"

"Your blood went missing from my workshop. Have you any enemies, my lady? I fear someone may be trying to do you harm."

"Show me."

Salizar led her to a locked glass cabinet at the edge of his row of oddities. The left pane was busted, revealing a tray of blood vials within. An undeft hand, then. Not a practiced thief.

Six tubes remained in the cabinet. "How did they know which blood was mine?"

Salizar swallowed. "The tube had your initials on it. To help me keep track."

Kara groaned.

"Forgive me, but you seem unsurprised."

Kara pasted on a smile. She'd decided against telling him about the shadow attack. It was possible he'd been involved. "It seems I really must stop flirting with Viscount Kendrick. I didn't know the debutantes would go to such lengths."

Salizar didn't laugh.

"You left some things out about your potion, by the way."

Salizar's eyes skittered away from hers. "Did I?"

Kara yanked up her blouse, exposing the dark stain spreading across her midriff. "Didn't think to mention this?"

Salizar's eyes shot open. He fell to his knees in front of her and raised a shaking hand, reaching out to caress the mark. Kara struggled to keep from recoiling.

"That spread…very quickly." His voice was almost reverent.

"Is that bad?"

"On the contrary, it means it was very effective. How do you feel?"

"Like shit."

"Then it's working."

"You won't be getting anymore blood from me, since you can't be trusted to keep it safe."

Salizar pursed his lips. "How about we revisit that when you need another dose?"

"You haven't held up your end of the bargain. I've been practicing the runes."

"What? Oh, right. Very busy, I'm afraid. To be honest, most who feign interest do not follow through."

"We made a deal. And I've been studying."

"Right." His lips curled into another smile that didn't meet his eyes. "Shall we practice now?"

Kara had her dreaded meeting with Thomas in the Belfry tonight, but otherwise her day was clear. She nodded.

"Which rune did you practice? Something simple, I hope. The power in your blood is diluted because of the demon's drip, so more advanced ones won't work."

Ah, the second catch. Kara had memorized half the book

already, but he didn't need to know that. "The one for unlocking."

"Good, good. I have something we can practice on." Salizar rummaged in the cabinet beneath his lab equipment for a minute before drawing out a small metal lockbox.

Kara borrowed one of Salizar's daggers to prick her finger on rather than reveal she was armed. She wiped the tip clean on her forearm, and Salizar rolled his eyes.

"Use your blood to draw the rune on the box. For a simple rune like this, painting it using one continuous stroke is best. You don't want any breaks in the line—you'll end up lighting something on fire rather than warming it that way. Sometimes yourself."

Kara traced the shape of the unlocking rune onto the box with the blood pooling on the tip of her finger. When she reached the end of the shape, her skin vibrated against the metal. The box popped open with a satisfying click. There were a few pungent dried herbs nestled inside.

"Very good. Clean, effective. Not that it was particularly challenging." Salizar snapped the lid shut and relocked it. "Now that your rune is on the box, you can unlock it again by reactivating the rune with a bit of fresh blood. No need to redraw it."

Kara tried it, squeezing out a fresh drop of blood and touching the rune. The lid popped open again.

"Some blood mages carry around vials of their blood so they don't have to bleed themselves all the time, but that's lazy. A good way to lose your blood to someone else and end up being their human power source. Never forget that your blood is your power. Scars are nothing to be afraid of. My master barely had an inch of scarless skin on his body by the time he died."

Kara chewed her lip. Hopefully her assailant had used all of her blood on the shadow spirit.

Salizar shut the lockbox and bent to put it back in the cabinet, and Kara snatched it out of his hands. She carried it to the sink beside his bubbling potions table and wet her sleeve with some water, using it to scrub her blood off the box. She'd have to burn this shirt later.

Salizar broke into a cackle. "You're learning."

"Whose grimoire did you give me, by the way? It's full of notes and customizations."

"An old copy that was found in the castle. There're no notes in it, though. Have you been defacing my book?"

Kara frowned. "I must have been mistaken." Had he given her the wrong grimoire by accident, or was he unable to see the notes for some reason? She'd have to inspect it further.

( )

NIGHT FELL UPON THE CASTLE, and Kara made her way to the belfry, dread creeping through her stomach. The bell tower shot up toward the sky like a megalith on the horizon. There were no guards outside, and someone had snuffed all the lights along the path. Either the servants or whoever awaited Kara in the darkness.

She kept her right hand on the hilt of her dagger as she walked through the tower's awning entrance. She didn't want to stab Thomas, but she was prepared to defend herself if he wanted a fight. Would he have backup? Darkness closed around her as she walked deeper within the stone edifice. The door slid shut behind her with a shudder.

Kara scanned the shadows for movement, but her night vision was weaker since she'd taken the demon's drip.

Shadows crowded around her, and she hunched her shoulders.

Someone circled her. She could sense them lurking in the shadows, just out of reach, but her body moved like mud when they lunged at her.

Hands grabbed her out of the darkness, wrapping around her mouth. Her scream came too late.

Hard warmth surrounded her, blocking her arms. Lips brushed against her ear.

"This isn't how I'd imagined our reunion."

Logan. She resisted the urge to melt against him in relief.

"You smell different," he growled against her ear. "I don't like it."

She squirmed against his hold, and he released her. She hated herself for wishing he'd held on longer.

"Having to resort to accosting women in the dark already?"

"As I recall, you were invited."

"I came to meet Thomas. I wouldn't have come if I thought you'd be here."

"I know."

"Why *are* you here, Logan?"

"I heard your conversation with Serena. When you were planning to tell me you'd been attacked? That your identity was compromised?"

"I'm surprised you took notice over the princess's chortling."

His shadow stopped circling her. "You're jealous." He had the audacity to sound genuinely surprised.

"I'm *angry.*"

"Because she rode your horse?" he scoffed.

Rage boiled up in her chest, clean and pure. "You insult me, Vakarian."

"I don't know what game you're playing, Kara. Jon's lucky to be alive. If I'd been keening—"

"But you've already taken care of that, haven't you?"

Logan drug his fingers through his hair.

Good, he was flustered.

"What are you talking about? I rode like hell across the Karashae for you, because I promised you I'd make it back. I didn't make that promise lightly, Kara. And when I returned, not only did you not recognize me—you asked a complete stranger to keen with you. Then I find you half-naked in my best friend's lap, kissing him?" His voice was ragged.

"Oh, I'm sorry I didn't recognize *Lord Melbourne* with the beard, the fake accent, and the mask covering his entire face."

"I knew you from the moment you walked in the room."

Kara despised the tingle that ran through her. "I didn't expect you to come back at all after what I saw! I had to figure out something." Some part of her subconscious had to have recognized him, but maybe she hadn't wanted to acknowledge how inescapable her feelings for him were.

Logan moved toward her. Kara stepped backward and ran into a bench. She resisted the urge to reach out into the darkness and touch him.

"What did you see, Kara? Who have you been spying on?"

If he accused her of being disloyal to the clan, she would stab him where he stood.

"You kissed her. Or she kissed you, but you did nothing to stop it, Logan." Her voice broke on the words, her chest heaving from the struggle to hold it all in.

His breath faltered. "How?"

"Serena loaned me a lover's bowl to scry for you in."

Logan cursed. "Well, that explains some things."

"This isn't funny, Logan." He'd shattered her. She never wanted to give anyone that power again.

"Darling, please let me explain." He stepped toward her, and she had nowhere to go. His heat crowded around her.

He reached for her, and she flinched. He hissed through his teeth and stepped back to allow her more space.

"Fuck," he growled. "She flirted with me from the moment we collected her. I paid it no mind, hoping she'd grow tired of it. It's not unusual—sheltered noble girl looking to rebel wants to cavort with the dangerous mercenary. Looking for one last gasp of excitement before they saddle themselves to a sedate noble for the rest of their lives. I ignored it. It was bloody annoying. I think she knew I had eyes for another, and that made her all the more determined. The princess is unaccustomed to not getting what she wants.

She complained about her impending betrothal to Prince Rand. How she'd never been kissed and would like to try it before being locked in for life. Jon offered to kiss her, of course. Hell, half the party did, even Faedra, but at that point she had it stuck in her mind. The game was too easily won if it wasn't me, as I'm the only one who told her no."

Kara had expected to be mad at Logan's recounting, but she just felt hollow. If she hadn't broken out Wesley— hadn't been kicked out of the clan to begin with, she would have been with them.

"She was growing bolder, and I—well, she's still the princess of the realm. Could be queen one day. I couldn't tell her to go to the goddess with the livelihood of the clan currently riding on Calim's contracts. When she came into the tent that night, I was bloody sick of it. I thought if I let her take her one kiss, she'd be satisfied. So I let her do it. It meant nothing to me, Kara. It was flesh, pressure. Air. *You. You mean everything to me.*"

"What happened next?"

"Your little bowl didn't tell you that?"

"Ask that to my doorframe."

Logan grunted. "When she didn't stop after one kiss, I stopped her myself and removed her from my tent, much to her disgruntlement. I asked Jon to sleep in my tent with me for the rest of my trip, just so she didn't get any ideas. She was beginning to piss me off, and I wanted to maintain the peace. He'll attest to that."

"If that's true, why are you humoring her now? You looked *through* me last night, Logan."

"I have a role to play, Kara. Just like you. And I was still fuming, trying to get over my anger. *Marriage mart?*"

"It was Serena's idea. It's not as if I actually intend to marry anyone."

Logan's voice went rough, low. Thunder rippled along his throat. "Why did you kiss him?"

Kara worried her thumbs across the tips of her nails. "I wanted to punish you. I wanted comfort, something to cling to while it felt like everything was crumbling around me. I thought I'd lost you—that I'd been a fool to think I ever had you."

"You've had me since Liore."

Her hands strained to touch him. She curled her fingers into her fists until nails bit flesh.

"He loves you, you know." It sounded like it'd torn something from Logan to say it.

Kara swallowed her spit.

"Do you love him?" Red eyes flickered in the darkness.

"Not in the way you mean." *Not like you.* She didn't dare

say the words aloud. Thing were too tenuous, too fragile to shake with the weight of that confession.

Logan shifted on his feet. She felt his desire to touch her like a palpable, living thing.

"You should have told me, Logan."

"I know. Things happened so fast when I got back—but that's no excuse, Kara. There is no excuse. I'm sorry. I never meant to hurt you. I wish I could fix it, fix *us*."

A horrible thought occurred to her, creeping into her mind like a worm.

"Did you tell her about me?"

Logan stilled. "What do you mean?"

"Did you tell her you were with someone? That you had someone waiting on you? Did you try and dissuade her with that?"

He shook his head no in the darkness, and the flame of hope inside her died. She bit the inside of her mouth until she tasted blood, trying to hold back her tears.

"What can I do, Kara? Please tell me what I can do."

"I need time."

"There are things we need to talk about. The keening…"

"I have it under control."

"Are you going to kill, then?"

"That won't be necessary."

Both irises lit with fire and blazed down at her. "If you think I will stand by and let another have you while your body—your heart—still burns for me, you are sorely mistaken."

"You're under the assumption that my body still burns for you."

Logan jerked her toward him, pulling her flush against his corded muscle. Hot awareness shot through her body, demon's drip be damned. *I guess that answers that question.*

His big hands skimmed the bones of her waist beneath her shirt, and she was grateful for the dark.

"You mean if I dove my hand into your leathers right now, you wouldn't be soaking wet for me?" His hands slid down her back and squeezed the cheeks of her ass, pulling her against the hard proof of his desire. "That if I bent you over this bench and fucked you, you wouldn't come on my cock and beg for more?"

Kara's sex clenched with desire that pulsed like a second heartbeat. He had the ability to make her go from rational thought to *sex, sex, sex* in seconds flat.

Sudden light pierced the darkness, and a gnarled voice called out, "I'm all for young love, but you'll have to find someplace else. I'm locking up." The bell attendant hobbled up the entranceway, toting a large torch. The play of light and shadow lit the craggy lines of his face with a wicked glow.

Logan pulled her into his chest, hiding her face from the man.

"This isn't over," he whispered into her ear. He pulled his cloak off, draped it over her head, and nudged her toward the door. Then he faded into the darkness.

CHAPTER EIGHT

Kara joined the training group in the palace courtyard in the morning, eager to work out some of her sexual frustration. The morning air was humid and thick with the promise of afternoon rain. Pippa and Tanith were there, clustered around a table laden with refreshments, which meant the princess was likely not far behind. Aidan led a group of soldiers through a set of drills on the far side of the yard, but Kara felt his gaze drift to her when she arrived.

Kara moved to a free spot on the grass and started stretching. She'd underestimated the effect the demon's drip would have on her. Her appetite was shit, and she woke up in the middle of the night nauseous and drenched in cold sweat. The toll of the last few days was wearing on her, dragging her down.

Kara bent to touch her toes and exhaled roughly as a sharp pain lanced through her abdomen. She scrunched her eyes against the discomfort and slowly unfolded. So much for her warmup.

Pippa and a tall Vespertine with short-cropped black

hair paired off with practice staves, and Kara watched them as she stretched her arms. Pippa was surprisingly deft with the longstaff, lunging and darting on sprightly feet. Thomas would like her.

Logan and Jon walked into the courtyard together, and Kara breathed a sigh of relief. They must be on speaking terms again. Logan wore a sleeveless leather jerkin that bared his arms today. He and Jon squared off with swords—wooden ones, thank the goddess. The bunch of Logan's tan, silken muscles and the nimble motions of his wrist as he swung his sword were hypnotizing. Kara caught herself biting her lip and forced her eyes away from him.

Princess Ariana had joined Tanith by the refreshments. She wore tight-fitted buckskin breeches and a smart blue tailcoat with golden buttons. She pulled on a pair of kidskin gloves and gestured for a soldier to pass her her weapon.

"Lady Grey," Ariana called out. "You look unoccupied. How about a friendly duel? I've heard you're decent with a blade."

"Truly, I'm not. I'd embarrass myself."

"Pish-posh," Pippa said as her bout with the Vespertine ended. "I've seen you out here, Celine!

"Are you calling my friends liars, then?" Ariana asked.

Kara looked to the sky and breathed through her nose. "Very well."

Normally she'd be concerned that her bloodlust would get the better of her in a fight with Ariana, but today she was just so *tired*. Her eyelids felt like they had tiny weights attached to them, dragging them down.

Kara picked a blunted practice sword from the rack by the refreshment table and moved to a clear spot in the yard. Ariana took her time of it, meandering over as she half-watched Logan and Jon's duel before finally crossing her blade with Kara's.

Kara blinked. The princess's sword was made of bright metal and battle sharp. Ariana's blue eyes glinted as she stepped in to swing.

Kara dodged, but her timing was off. She felt like she was wading through water. Ariana continued her attacks, quick and precise. She'd been well-trained. Kara parried her with ease, but when she saw an opening in the princess's defenses, she only tapped Ariana with the tip of her sword. They'd probably hang her from the ramparts if she drew royal blood.

As Kara scored more taps, Ariana's swings grew more reckless. Kara dodged the blade going straight for her gut, and the twist of her abdomen burned like fire. Her face contorted in a wince.

Ariana saw it, and she capitalized on the weakness, aiming most of her strikes at Kara's abdomen and legs. Kara dodged another gut shot, and Ariana followed it up with a wild swing at her face. Kara faltered, a moment too slow, stunned by the princess's eagerness to do her harm. She wasn't even pretending at caution. Kara drew her left forearm up at the last second to block the swing, and the sword bit into her.

Kara cried out in pain. She dropped her sword and clutched her arm, backing away from Ariana as blood began to spill over her fingers.

The entire courtyard went still, watching.

"Oh goddess. I'm so sorry. I assumed you were more skilled than you are. I should have been more careful." The glee in the princess's eyes didn't fade. Her sword was streaked red with Kara's blood.

"I think I've had enough for the day."

Logan waited on the sidelines, his face tight. His eyes tracked her like a hawk.

Kara walked into the shade of an overhanging balcony and examined her arm. The cut wasn't too deep, but it stung like the mother and bled freely. Her stomach was a big ball of writhing knots. Sweat stuck to her skin, and Kara glared up at the sun wavering in the sky. She was going to start banning Merry from waking her before noon.

Logan crossed the yard to her, his face intent. Jon lingered behind, though he tossed her a smile when their eyes met.

"Are you alright?"

Sweat streaked down his arms and the vee of his neck, glittering atop his skin.

Kara forced herself to tear her gaze away. "Are you deigning to speak to me in public now?"

Logan's brow furrowed. "We were both angry. I don't want us to be angry with each other anymore."

Kara rolled her eyes. "Before today I thought I was the bloodthirsty one."

"Oh trust me, you are."

"You didn't bring Bart along, did you?"

Logan shook his head. "Bart asked for a vacation before we left for Travincal. Blackhearth will be rubble by the time we return if he and Aethyta decide to make-up for the twentieth time."

We return. Hope swelled in Kara's chest, but she clenched it off, stuffing it down. Hope was disappointment in the making.

"Do you need stitches?"

"It's a scratch. I'll be fine."

Logan looked at her arm doubtfully.

The extent of the wound was obscured by her sleeve,

but a trail of blood had streaked down to the cuff, staining it red. It was far deeper than a scratch, but Kara wasn't interested in his help or the shame of admitting she needed it. Maybe she could heal it herself with a rune from the grimoire.

"What's going on? Are you sick? Your reactions were so slow out there."

"I'm *playing a role.*"

Logan's frown turned severe. "I don't for a second believe you'd willingly let the princess draw blood, role or no role. You're not that good an actor."

He wasn't wrong. It rankled her that Ariana had gotten the better of her. "Perhaps your estimation of my skills is flawed."

Logan scoffed. "Please, before we left Raven's Rest you could hold your own with me."

A quiet pleasure curled through her at his compliment.

Viscount Kendrick appeared behind Logan, her unlikely hero. Kara smiled brightly at him. "Aidan. I'll have to stick to sparring with you in the future."

"I've no idea why she was using a real sword—that was uncalled for."

He looked between her and Logan, and recognition dawned in his eyes. "Is this man bothering you?"

"No," Logan said at the same time Kara said, "Yes."

"His conversation is dreadful. I think I need to go have a rest."

"Would you like an escort to the healer?"

"I'll take her," Logan said. He turned his back to Kara and stepped forward, blocking her almost entirely from Aidan's view.

"She asked you to leave, Vakarian."

"Enough! I shall attend to myself."

. . .

Kara returned to her rooms, utterly spent despite it not yet being midday. A jeweled tray holding a thick invitation card awaited her on the vanity. Kara flipped it open.

Meet me in the library today.
    -C

Kara groaned. She had little to tell Calim of besides how she'd misplaced her blood and enabled a spell that nearly got her killed by her own shadow. It'd been close to a month since she arrived. How long until he took her off the contract entirely? Would he demand she repay her wages? Kara hadn't spent them yet, but they were her only contingency plan if she didn't rejoin the Brotherhood, which seemed more and more likely lately.

Kara dressed her arm with a strip of silk torn from one of her slips and changed into a fresh shirt, then headed for the library.

Voices carried from within when she arrived. She paused outside the doors.

"If you want his ships and soldiers so badly, you marry him. I refuse to be the crown's broodmare. Look where that got grandmama."

Ariana. She must have left after their duel. Their grandmother was Queen Genevieve, the woman King Urian had married to conceive a royal heir when Namirah was his consort. When he'd eventually shunned Namirah for Genevieve, it'd set off the trail of events that led to Namirah's curse and the beginning of the Curse Wars.

"I thought we had an understanding, sister."

"Maybe when I was fifteen and dumb to the ways of

the world. What of your obligation to the crown? It's been years, and you're still pining for that commoner."

"You talk of things you don't understand."

"Oh, I understand perfectly, but you're the bloody king. Act like it for once instead of foisting your responsibilities on me."

"At least agree to meet him, Ari. I won't force you into a marriage, but the wolves are at our heels."

"Fine. Invite him. But prepare to be disappointed."

Angry footsteps neared the door, and Kara quickly stepped away and began walking down the hall at a relaxed pace. The library doors swung open with a thud, and the princess stormed past Kara without slowing.

Kara waited until she disappeared around the corner, then returned to the library.

Calim sat in his usual chair by the farthest hearth, head bowed in his hands. He wore a black doublet with a golden leaf design stitched down the sleeves today. It made him look regal.

Kara cleared her throat as she approached.

Calim sat up. "Lady Grey. I didn't expect you so soon."

Kara curtsied. "I can return later if you wish."

"No, no. You're fine."

"Have you asked me here for a report?"

Calim rose a finger to his lips and moved toward the hearth that flickered with green spellfire. Then he stepped into the flames.

Kara's jaw dropped, her scream stuck in her throat. Calim didn't even flinch.

He stepped out of the flames into the backside of the hearth and beckoned for her to follow. "Come. It doesn't burn like true fire."

Kara stepped towards the hearth and stretched a hand out over the wicked green blaze. She jerked when the spellfire licked at her skin. It emanated the warm glow of an actual fire, but the flames were icy cold to the touch.

Kara took a breath and stepped into the hearth. Cold caressed her, fluttering against her skin. It was like walking through a tiny upside down blizzard. The cold abated as soon as she stepped free of the flames. The back of the hearth was large, tall enough for her and Calim to stand without hunching. "Well. That's something."

Calim pointed to a small rune etched into the back wall of the hearth. It was tiny, hard to see from this angle. Kara bent to inspect it and smiled.

Unlock. But why was the king using blood runes to hide his secret passageways? Perhaps Salizar had set them up.

"We need a bit of blood to unlock it. It's a blood rune."

Kara swiped a finger under the strip of silk on her arm, already stained a bright red from the cut that refused to clot. She probably had the demon's drip to thank for that as well.

She traced her finger along the shallow curves of the rune, and the stone wall to the right rumbled open.

Calim sucked in a breath.

Kara tilted her head up to him. "Have you not been back here before?"

"It's been a long time." His dark eyes danced with the spellfire's green gleam.

Kara stood and gestured to the shadowed doorway they'd unsealed. "After you."

She followed Calim into a full-sized room. A cluster of older style fae lanterns floated on the ceiling, emitting a warm amber light. An enormous bedframe took up the center of the room. It was four-postered, with a full canopy, and the dark wooden bedposts were so thick with carved runes that there was hardly any bare wood remaining. The bedframe itself was stripped of mattress and bedding.

Kara raised her brows. The rest of the room was equally barren. Several empty bookcases spanned the walls, and a large picture frame covered in a dark cloth rested in the far corner.

"Your former sex dungeon?" Kara asked.

Calim burst into a laugh. "One of Urian's." He ran his palm over a rune beside the entranceway, and the rock wall slid back into place, sealing them in.

Kara's stomach twisted. She didn't like being trapped within the palace's walls. She'd much rather be atop one of the spires, where at least there was a quicker escape available than a slow death by starvation.

"Who stayed here?" The energy of the room was odd, discordant. Anger bled from the walls and pressed in around her. Someone had spent a lot of time in here, judging by the extent of the runework, yet it'd been stripped of all personal affect.

"This was one of Namirah's rooms."

Kara swallowed.

"Her and Urian met in secret here after he married my grandmother. I've found a few like it around the palace—some empty, some entirely black from fire. I'm sure there are more I've yet to discover."

Kara summoned an image of the old king leaving the bed of his wife and stealing through the flames to join the arms of his lover, hidden within the palace walls. Namirah's rage still tainted this place. It was a glorified cell.

"Sometimes I'd hide in here as a boy, when I managed to escape my tutors, but the place always frightened me. It doesn't see much use of late."

Kara brushed against a stray cobweb and shivered. "It is rather sinister."

"I thought we could discuss your progress in here, away from prying eyes and ears."

"I'm afraid I've little to report. Lord Rutherford isn't a fan of your governing style, but you likely knew that already, as he's not shy with his opinions. I haven't found evidence of any treason yet. And your sister doesn't much care for me." An understatement, considering Kara was still bleeding from their last encounter.

Kara expected anger, but Calim just nodded. "I didn't expect this would be easy. The courtiers are a cliquish lot, wary of outsiders. I'll see if I can pull some strings for you. I know it's difficult, but do what you can to get in Ari's good graces. She's always been the one the people look to for their cues."

"How much do you trust Salizar?" Kara hadn't ruled out him casting the shadow spell and faking the stolen blood break-in.

"He's been with us a long time. I paid for his schooling at the mage college in Temodor. I wouldn't usually suspect him, but rule out no one. Sanguine pockets run deeper than the crown's these days."

Kara ran a finger across one of the bookshelves, dragging a line through the dust.

"Is your involvement with Vakarian jeopardizing your progress?"

Kara's heart stuttered. "We have no involvement."

"I wasn't born yesterday, Lady Grey. I was at the ball."

"It's over."

Calim sighed. "Right. Serena told me of the attempt on your life. Have you recovered? Forgive me for saying so, but you look unwell."

Bloody demon's drip. "I'm alright. And for whatever reason, the assailant hasn't revealed my identity to the court yet, so I'm not fully compromised."

Calim nodded. "I'm willing to keep you in the game, but do you want to continue, despite the risk to your life? I'm not a cruel man. If you want to pull out, let me know. You could keep everything you've earned thus far."

With her current savings, Kara could leave and afford to settle someplace new, away from the danger and the Stygians. But she'd be running away, just like she had with Wesley. Here, she had something, even if it was complicated. Out there, she had nothing.

"I want to continue."

Calim took a breath and closed his eyes. "Very well. I confess that there's another reason I brought you here. You're marked, aren't you, Kara?"

Kara stilled. The king had never used her given name before. She thought he hadn't known it. "What did Vakarian tell you about me?"

"Nothing. You're not the only spy in my employ."

Kara lowered her head. Of course.

"Besides, I guessed the first time I saw you."

She narrowed her brow. "What do you mean?"

Calim crossed to the covered picture frame in the corner and pulled the cover off, revealing a portrait.

A raven-haired woman in a crimson dress filled the frame. She sat in a high-backed chair studded with rivets, one leg crossed over the other, her hands curled over the arms of the chair. Her dark eyes were hard and calculating within the fine bones of her cheeks. There was something disconcerting about the woman. Her face, the set of her eyes and sweep of her eyebrows over full lips made Kara's blood run cold. It was the face Kara saw in the mirror every day, traced over with an artist's dark brush strokes.

"The resemblance is uncanny, isn't it? You startled me when I first saw you."

Kara had forgotten Calim was in the room. She

pulled her eyes away from the subject's magnetic gaze, jerking as a shiver ran up her spine. She tossed her head to clear the needle-like pin-pricks running along her skin.

"Who is this?" Part of her already knew the answer, already denied it.

"Namirah. One of the few portraits that survived when Urian had everything of hers burnt."

"Is this some kind of trick?" Even as she asked, Kara knew it wasn't. The painting showed signs of age, and the frame's metal filigree was choked with dust.

"This portrait used to give me nightmares as a boy. All those tales of Namirah the curse bringer, Namirah the wretched. Sometimes when I came here, I thought I could hear her whispering my name. That if I stayed here after dark, she'd crawl out from under the bedframe and grab me by the ankles."

"And now?"

"Now I've gained...perspective."

"Why did you bring me here?"

"There have always been rumors that Urian and Namirah had a child. Why would Namirah curse Princess Laura, an innocent child, after all, rather than Urian or Genevieve?"

Trepidation curled inside her.

"But I never really believed it until I saw you."

Kara snorted. "You think—" She gestured between the portrait and her, at a loss for words.

"Not their child, no, you're too young for that. A grandchild, though. I've been looking into your late adoptive father."

Kara bristled, prepared to defend Da, even to the king of bloody Teleria.

"Caliban McKenna. He was no simple soldier, Kara.

He was one of Urian's personal guard. He might have cut down your parents himself."

"*No.*" Kara's mind rebelled at the idea. Da wouldn't.

"Perhaps he couldn't go through with his mission once faced with killing a wailing babe, so he fled his post and took you and his family halfway across the world. Hid in a hovel in the Balmoran Mountains for twenty years. I received a letter from the man I sent to Mudbottom to investigate this week. The story's a little too convenient, isn't it? Baby on a wagon full of goods, parents lost to the battle moments before they could escape. Your parents were probably the reason the town was invaded to begin with."

Kara shook her head violently. She felt like the world was crumbling out from under her. "That proves nothing. Those are just theories. Hypotheticals."

Calim's face slid into something halfway between a smile and a grimace. "Kara, that blood rune outside is keyed to only open to royal blood and Namirah's."

A boulder dropped into Kara's stomach. The roar of Widow's Fall thundered through her ears. She sank to the floor and pressed her hands to her face. He was wrong. He had to be wrong.

Kara lifted her head, hope surging through her as she hit upon an idea. "Maybe I'm a distant relation from somewhere else in the line. Hell, even your parents might've had some hidden bastards." And she'd taken the demon's drip. There was no telling whose blood was in it.

Calim shook his head and began pacing the room. "My parents were a love match, and they died young. And you're the spitting image of Namirah. I understand your reluctance to believe this, but I bear you no ill will. I've no interest in the so-called cleansing my grandfather perpetrated."

Kara had grown accustomed to not knowing about her past, stopped hoping she'd learn something about her parents long ago. Da and Wesley were enough—had always been enough, before all this. It was easier that way. Far easier, if this was her dark legacy.

"I don't want this."

Calim nodded. "I don't expect anything of you, so you know. But I thought it important to make you aware. Some may seek to harm you for your connection to her, if it ever came to light. And maybe you were…curious, about your past?"

Kara pressed her palms into her eyelids until spots swam in her vision.

"It's a past tainted with blood and vengeance." History was always trying to repeat itself. Had Urian kept track of his illegitimate child and cleansed them along with everything else of Namirah's?

"You need time to adjust. This is a lot. I'll give you some space." Calim rubbed her on the shoulder and left the room, and the walls seemed to shrink in on her.

The idea that she could be related to Namirah, to the *late king*, seemed ludicrous. She glanced up at the portrait again, fighting the shiver that rolled down her spine. It was the eyes. They glittered like the edge of a knife, promising violence. Is that what her eyes looked like when the bloodlust took over? Utterly without warmth?

She forced herself to look away, gaze going to the runed bedposts instead. The hurried strokes were vaguely familiar. The rune for *search* had been carved into the wood over and over again, the shape and strokes growing cramped as she ran out of space. What had Namirah been searching for? Kara's eyes widened in recognition of rune variations matching those in the marginalia of her grimoire. The same grimoire Salizar claimed had nothing written in it. That he'd found in the palace.

Mother Night. Kara scuttled backwards toward the door, swiping her hand across the stone until it found the impressions of the rune to open the doorway. The stone groaned as it slid open. Kara fled back through the icy flames.

The library was empty when she returned. She paused to collect herself, then took the opportunity to draw a few eavesdropping runes throughout the room, under rugs and lamps and even inside a few books. On the way back to her room, she stopped by the garden and collected a few smooth stones to key the runes to.

CHAPTER NINE

Kara spent the next two days in a haze of sleep and drink, trying to quell the creeping sense of dread Namirah's room and Calim's theory had seeded in her.

Her eavesdropping runes weren't working, making her entire plan to take her mind off Calim's revelations and make progress on her mission a bust. The stones she'd keyed to the runes had yet to glow or rattle or produce any noise whatsoever, even when she refreshed her blood on them. They must require more power than she was producing whilst on the demon's drip.

She'd expected the potion's side effects to ease off by now, but if anything, they'd gotten worse. The mark crept steadily across her abdomen. The upper edge of the black sunburst had reached the middle of her ribcage, and it showed no signs of stopping. She began concealing the dark circles crowding her eyes with face powder from the vanity. She was losing weight, too. Her dresses sagged on her frame, and no matter how much she ate at meals, a gnawing hunger persisted in the pit of her belly.

Kara hated feeling so weak, but she was well into the time her keening should have started with none of the usual signs—none of the fine-edged tilting into anger or lust at a moment's notice. Logan still heated her blood, but at least she wasn't beholden to the curse. Had Logan's keening begun yet? Had he already sated it with another? The thought made her itch to hit something.

She wanted to confide in him about Calim's theory, but staying removed was the only way to avoid getting sucked back into his maelstrom. He would destroy her if she let him.

Kara stared out her bedroom window and watched the sun set on the seven spires, another unproductive day come to its end. She imagined she was a feather floating from the top of a spire down through the air currents, lower and lower, until she settled on the surface of the lake. She wanted to sink. She'd become a player in someone else's game. Believing Calim felt disloyal to Da—like she was besmirching his memory, but the king's claims were hard to refute.

Kara carried her glass and carafe of wine to the bathroom and began filling the bathtub with hot water. She sprinkled a sachet of sandalwood-scented powder into the tub, and colored bubbles unfurled across the water's surface. She let the tub fill till it was nearly overflowing, dropped her robes on the floor, and stepped in. Excess water sloshed over the edges as she sunk down into the water's warm embrace. She submerged her shoulders, then her head, until only her nose was exposed. She stayed like that for several minutes. Dark echoes filled her ears as the water wrapped around her. She wished she could sink into this tub and float up somewhere else, in some nameless pond, in some nameless place.

Kara lifted her head from the water and forced her

eyes open. Steam filled the bathroom, and the musky notes of the bath powder filled the air. There was a dull thud as someone knocked on the door to the bedroom.

"Come in," Kara called. Merry must have forgotten something earlier, but she wasn't about to get out of the tub.

The outer door snicked open and closed, and then the bathroom door opened, letting in a draft of cold air.

"Shut the door." Kara hunched forward and closed her eyes, trying to block out the cold and hide the mark on her stomach.

"Have you any talent for massage? I'm miserably sore." Her shoulders were bunched into tight knots, and the arm Ariana had sliced open ached when she tried to stretch it. Even the shoulder Patch had put an arrow through, long healed, was bothering her since she'd started the demon's drip.

A shadow fell over Kara as Merry stepped forward. She gathered Kara's hair and slid it in front of her shoulders. Prickles tickled Kara's skin as the expanse of her back was exposed to the air. Warm, calloused hands gripped her shoulders and began to knead. Kara let out an involuntary moan as fingers dug into knotted flesh.

Kara let go of her knees and let her head hang forward as Merry traced behind her ears and down her neck. Strong thumbs began working their way along the column of her spine. Relaxed heat flowed through her muscles. The hands trailing the length of her spine dipped beneath the water and began rubbing the dimples above her butt. It felt divine, but it was odd for Merry to be so forward. And so quiet.

Kara tilted her head back, and Logan's glowing amber eyes stared down at her.

Kara shrieked and nearly jumped out of the tub. "What are you doing here?!"

Logan smirked. "You told me to come in."

"I thought you were my maid!"

He let out a dark laugh. "Does your maid have hands like this?" He slid his hands around her back and cupped her breasts in his large paws. He tweaked her nipples, and heat whipped through Kara. She wanted to wrap her hands around his neck and pull him down to her lips, to pull him into the tub with her and coat the floor in water with their frantic movements. No, no, this wasn't supposed to be happening. She was on the bloody demon's drip. Kara whined in the back of her throat and slapped the top of the water with her hands.

"You seem frustrated," he murmured in her ear. His hot breath against the bare skin of her neck sent a wave of heat through her. The ache between her thighs built.

One of his hands slid lower, fingers spread across the taut skin of her stomach. The thick layer of bubbles atop the water hid the black sun staining her skin. Logan paused as he reached the apex of her thighs, asking her a question. He caught her earlobe between his teeth and sucked. Kara's sex pulsed in response, her hips lifting slightly. A low growl filled her ear.

"Let me give you this. It will help relieve your tension."

Against her better judgment, Kara spread her knees in invitation.

His fingers slid between her legs and slowly traced her folds, spreading her slickness around before settling on her clit. Kara tossed her head back, and he caught her lips with his. His kiss was hard and full of need. Kara wrapped her hands around the edges of the tub as pleasure rocked through her. Her knees slipped against the sides as her hips lifted to meet his hand eagerly, splashing water over the edge.

She moaned into his mouth. He wrapped his hand around her neck, pinning her there so he could devour her, and it turned her on even more.

Pleasure dripped through her as his fingers circled her clit in slow motions. Then his hand dipped lower, and he slid two fingers inside her, curling them against a sensitive spot deep within.

Kara sucked his lower lip between her teeth and groaned. She was out of control. She was supposed to be mad at him, not writhing beneath his hand. She was already on the verge of orgasm. Logan's thumb stroked her clit as his fingers curled inside her, rubbing that secret place, and it sent her over the edge. She came, shuddering beneath his hand and clenching around his fingers.

"You're driving me insane," he groaned. His eyes were yellow orbs—he was full on keening. He brushed her oversensitized clit once more, and she jerked in his arms.

Logan scooped his arms beneath her knees and back and lifted her out of the water. His shirt was soaked through from her splashing and wet skin. Water dripped off her back into the tub. Logan's gaze drifted across her naked body, hunger in his eyes.

Kara was slow to remember the dark mark from the demon's drip, still languishing in the heady aftermath of her orgasm. Then her brain caught up, and she tried to twist out of his arms before he saw, but he held her tight against him.

His eyes froze on the violent black streaks that spread across her abdomen. His fingers dug into her flesh. "*What is that?*" His voice shook.

Kara lowered her eyes. The game was up. "I got a new tattoo?"

Logan carried her away, kicking the bathroom door open, and dropped her on the bed. "Start talking."

Kara reached for the sheet to cover herself, and Logan yanked it out of her hand. "Now's hardly the time for modesty, Kara. Not when I've kissed every inch of you."

Kara's cheeks flushed. "It's nothing you need to worry about. I'm fine."

Logan began to pace and wrung his hands through his hair. "You've lost weight, you're pale, that cut you got three days ago is still open when it should have closed already. You smell like—like corruption. Oh, and you have a bloody shadow spreading beneath your skin that wasn't there a month ago. You're clearly not *fine*, and I will not stand by and watch you hurt yourself."

"It's none of your business. I have it under control."

"Did it start after your shadow attacked you? Someone is obviously trying to harm you, and you won't talk to me about it. Please let me help."

She didn't owe him an explanation. When had he ever offered her one?

Logan's face fell. "You don't trust me."

"You lost that privilege when you let another woman kiss you. But this is unrelated to the attack." *As far as she knew.*

His expression turned thunderous. "Tell me what it is, or I will lock you in this room until you do."

"But the contract—"

"I don't give a fuck about the contract, Kara. I owed Serena a favor after she saved you, and now we're both stuck in this godsforsaken palace with that willful brat."

"Protecting the princess is the favor?" Warmth spread through her chest. So it was just a job after all. Though the clan would be displeased if they weren't making any money off it.

Logan gave a short nod. "The escort and your contract were already set up, but we weren't supposed to stick around afterward."

Would he really lock her in here? She wouldn't put it past him… She could use the unlocking rune, but she had a feeling he meant to lock himself in with her. By the flintiness of his stare, he wasn't going to let it go anytime soon.

Kara sighed. "I heard a rumor that a local mage was working on an antidote for the monthly keening. I had no plans to take it at first, but after what I saw in the lover's bowl, and then the masque and the hunt… I didn't want to be beholden to anything this month, especially you."

"Your eyes… I haven't seen Namirah's fire in your eyes since the feast. Was it Serena?" he asked in a low voice.

Kara shook her head.

"Who?" His eyes were going red, and Kara shoved her hands beneath her legs so she wouldn't nervously pick at her fingers. If Logan got to Salizar, she'd never get another dose out of him. Assuming he survived to make more.

"Why are you protecting them?! Whatever they gave you is poisoning you, Kara. I've lived with the curse since I was eighteen—you think I haven't tried everything already? Every so-called cure and charm in Teleria and abroad? There is no remedy. Not even cutting the mark off —it will grow right back. Anything that works is worse than the curse itself, because the curse is a part of you. And it won't be suppressed. Not without taking you with it. Better to be stuck with your own demons."

"Maybe this new one works. I should be keening by now, but I haven't felt the usual impulses—"

Logan fanned his hand out over her abdomen, and Kara shrunk away from the dull pain.

"It's hurting you." Logan's frown deepened. "It feels wrong. Like the opposite of life. Show me what you took."

"There's none left."

"Do you have the container still?"

"In the armoire."

Logan dug through it, yanking out several dresses before surfacing with the bag. He uncorked the vial and sniffed it. His lips curled back, eyes gone crimson. A menacing rumble rolled out of his throat. *"Mancator magicae."*

"What?"

"Magic eater. Mother night." His eyes slid closed. "How long ago did you take this?"

Kara quickly counted backwards in her head. "Five days."

Logan's eyes swung towards her. "That's impossible. The amount of magic you'd have to have in your blood— How much of it did you take?"

"Just that vial. Have you tried it before?"

Logan nodded. "They had to cut it out of me before it strangled my heart, but I was on it for months. Yours is spreading way too quickly."

Kara paled. "Cut it out of you?" she whispered. She glanced down at the mark coating half her abdomen in mute horror.

Logan jerked his head in a nod.

Now really didn't seem like the best time to disclose that she might be the long-lost granddaughter of the woman responsible for their curse. But if it was true—*there was no way it was true*—it might be affecting the demon's drip.

"There's something else. Calim has this absurd theory that I'm related to Namirah."

Logan's eyes snapped open. *"What?"*

"There's a portrait of her in the library, looks like I sat for the damn thing. I think he's crocked, of course, but if there's a chance it's true…that could be why it spread so fast."

She relayed everything Calim had told her about Da and the keyed blood rune. Logan started pacing the room again, hands shoved deep into his pockets.

"Like I said, it's absurd."

"We can't rule out the possibility. If Namirah's power was passed down, it would explain the rate of growth. We need to talk to the mage who gave you the potion, Kara. Give me their name."

Kara ignored his demand. "Why would you have to cut it out of me? I thought it just went away on its own." Surely Salizar would have mentioned that.

"It's a parasite, Kara. The magic eater works by consuming the magic in your blood, suppressing the onset of your keening and the other strengths of the curse. Magic is an inextricable part of you—it's essentially feeding off your life force. With a weak enough host injecting them rarely, they die off before they do too much damage. They're not meant to be borne long-term."

He glanced down at her stomach. "To have spread this quickly though…it's like a thirsty man in the desert finding a bottomless jug of fresh, cold water. He'd bloat himself on it."

Kara blanched.

"And when they grow too large, their instinct is to kill their host so they can find another. They'll work their way through your bloodstream and wrap around your heart until it stops beating." Logan clenched his fist in the air for effect. "In the past, they've been used to harvest the magic of prisoners. If the magic eater is extracted alive, a mage can use all of the power it siphoned in their own spells."

She was going to kill Salizar. Had he known about her

link to Namirah, too? Or was it a happy accident for him? He'd been in awe when she showed him the mark.

Logan tugged her off the bed and led her to the mirror. He stood behind her, hands on her shoulders. "Watch closely."

Kara stared at the hollow of her stomach for several long seconds. She was about to look away when one of the dark tendrils writhed slightly and grew longer. Chills skittered over her skin like a thousand tiny insects. Nausea rose in the back of her throat.

"Get it out of me," she whispered.

"We can't do it here. The process will be…noisy. And painful. It will burn you from the inside out, Kara."

"How did you remove yours?"

"I got really drunk and fished it out with a knife. Wouldn't recommend. I was taking them for months, trying to outrun the keening, and my mark was half the size of yours. I won't lie to you. It's going to be excruciating."

Kara bit her lip. "There's a blood mage at court. Salizar. He gave it to me."

Logan's jaw ticked, his expression promising violence.. "We're going to pay him a visit."

"You can't kill him. He might be a lead on the Sanguines. He had a sample of my blood prior to the shadow mirror spell."

Logan cursed. "Take me to him."

Logan kicked down Salizar's door instead of knocking, and Kara jumped.

"What is the meaning—" Salizar's raised voice lowered as he saw who stood in his doorway.

"Oh good, you're in," Logan said. Ice ran through his words.

Salizar skittered behind his cauldron. "Lord Melbourne. Commander. What can I do for you?" His eyes slid from Logan to Kara, and he blanched a little.

Logan strode into the room like he owned it and motioned for Kara to follow.

"Show him," he growled.

Kara lifted her shirt, exposing the dark mark that crawled across her stomach. It was twice the size of when Salizar had seen it last.

Salizar's mouth gaped. He slowly circled the cauldron and approached her. "Beautiful." He raised a hand to touch the mark, and Logan snatched his wrist out of the air and squeezed until Salizar whimpered.

"Don't touch her. You got her into this mess, you get her out of it."

"I had a chance to finish analyzing my notes on your blood, from before it was stolen. Yours had several unusual markers. Who cast the sanguinata on you?"

Kara stilled. Salizar knew too much. "That's irrelevant."

"On the contrary, it could be why the demon's drip reacted so…vigorously. If my analysis was correct, you had the blood of a cursed male in your system. But that couldn't be right, could it?" Malice glinted in his eyes. "If you give me another sample, I can run more tests."

Logan slammed Salizar against the wall and lifted him by the neck. Several glass jars fell to the ground and broke open.

Kara winced at the thud his body made. Logan's eyes were dancing red at the edges, his usual control being tested by the keening. The urge to squeeze the life out of Salizar would be hard to resist.

"You're never getting your hands on her blood or that magic eater, mage. You're going to remove it in the most painless way possible, and your reward will be your life. For now."

Salizar's face was turning red, and his eyes had grown three times their usual size. He was staring at Logan like he'd seen a god. "It's you—the sanguinata," he sputtered. "A male Namirahn alive until adulthoood. Do you know how rare you are?" His voice came out in rasps as Logan's fingers tightened.

"Logan," Kara said as his shoulders spread, muscles bulging beneath his clothes. She laid a hand on his arm and squeezed. "We need him."

Logan dropped Salizar and tore across the room, putting distance between them. Salizar slid to the floor and massaged his bruised throat.

"I'll do it in exchange for your blood," he said to Logan.

"You will do it," Logan roared, and all the glass containers in the room shook, "Or I will eviscerate you and decorate the palace with your entrails."

Salizar struggled to his feet, eyes darting around the room. "Even with the sanguinata, that's unprecedented growth in such a brief span of time. Do you have any mages in your family?"

"No. More. Questions," Logan growled.

"I'm aware that you operate in matters of sword in, sword out, but I need to know the why before I can figure out the how."

A low rumble emanated from Logan's side of the room.

Salizar threw his hands up. "Bloody barbarians. This is why they kill you all in your cribs. Fine, we'll do it your way. But she asked for this, you know! I shouldn't be held accountable for her recklessness."

"If you don't stop talking, I am going to cut out your tongue. Piece. By. Piece."

Kara wiped her clammy hands off on her pants. Judging by Logan's anger, this was going to seriously suck.

Salizar cleared off a large work bench and gestured toward it. "The operating table." He pulled a tattered book out from under a shelf and began flipping through it.

Kara laid on top of the table and rolled up her shirt until the entire mark was exposed. Logan took her hand in his and rubbed his thumb across her knuckles. He looked scared.

"You can't do the spell to remove it?"

He shook his head. "It's beyond my knowledge. I might hurt you. The sanguinata… I'd never used it before. I only dared risk it because you were dying."

Kara gulped. She watched as Salizar drew a rune by the entrance to the room, one she recognized from the grimoire. It blocked sound from escaping a place. Her stomach churned.

"The strongest blood will have the greatest effect here. And hers is dampened at the moment." He looked pointedly at Logan.

"I'll do it." Logan took the wooden bowl Salizar offered and cut open his arm with his dagger, dripping blood into the bowl until it was half full.

Salizar dipped his fingers into the blood and tasted them, his eyes going bright. His expression was almost orgasmic.

Logan stabbed his knife into the wooden workbench, and it stuck in all the way to the hilt. "I will cut your fingers off if you do that again. You only need one."

Salizar rolled his eyes and muttered something under

his breath about Namirahns. He carried his grimoire to the workbench for reference and began painting runes onto Kara's abdomen. He was slow, methodical. At one point he fetched a fine paintbrush to draw the small connecting lines between each rune.

Kara grew more uneasy as she watched him work. Some runes she recognized from her grimoire, but others were arcane and unfamiliar. The outer runes circled the dark mark in an eight-pointed pattern, and the inner web was convoluted knotwork that reminded her of the lover's bowl.

Logan leaned on the edge of the workbench and held Kara's hand as Salizar worked, keeping a keen eye on the mage's design.

It took Salazar an hour to finish. Logan analyzed the finished runework for several minutes, tracing the lines with his eyes. "Why are you using a transport rune?"

Salizar let out an exacerbated huff. "Amateur runeworkers, think they know everything. It's to help transport the magic eater from inside her body to outside it without having to mangle her flesh with a knife, likely killing her in the process."

"If you try anything, mage, you will not live to regret it."

"She's going to need something to bite down on."

Logan's eyes shuttered.

Kara's heart started to race, and cold sweat pooled between her breasts. Logan unbuckled his dagger's leather scabbard from his belt and handed it to her. Kara slid the leather between her teeth. She was no stranger to pain, but the way they were acting was making her nervous. Just how bad did they expect it to be?

Salizar swiped his hands through the bowl of blood,

coating his palms with it, and held them over the runework. He began to chant in an arcane language.

Nothing happened at first. Then the mark moved. Dark tendrils writhed beneath her skin, the edges of the black sun dancing. Looking at it made her want to puke.

Salizar raised his hands and pulled his fingers back, like he was drawing something towards him.

The tendrils lifted, causing a raised ripple. It felt like someone was tugging beneath her skin with an invisible rope. The rope drew tighter and tighter, the tendrils moving faster as they struggled to escape his pull. There were a thousand tiny barbs beneath her skin, all scraping against each other.

The rope snapped. The tendrils pulsed, and a small sliver of darkness lifted from her skin. Every muscle in her body seized as fire whipped through her. She tossed her head back and bit hard into the leather, grinding her teeth down on it as she tried to get control. She expected her pain to plateau as her body adjusted, for it to gradually become more bearable, but it just kept rising.

The rest of the tendril lifted from her flesh, and her eyes rolled back in her head. Blood welled beneath her fingers where her nails cut into Logan's palm.

"Your body will want to pass out to manage the pain. I runed you to try and prevent it. It's better if you stay awake to fight."

Logan snarled, his eyes a menacing red. The eyes of a predator on their prey.

"Please stop. I'd rather live with it. Just make it stop."

Another lash of fire, and Kara's entire body jerked. She tried to roll away, to escape the horrible sensations.

Logan climbed on top of the table and pulled her head into his lap. His arms wrapped around hers, holding them still. He leaned forward and pressed his forehead against her sweat-soaked one. "I'm so sorry, but this has to happen, my love. It's killing you."

Kara locked her legs beneath the table's surface to keep from kicking out at Salizar.

Tears leaked down her face, and she screamed into the scabbard each time a tendril worked its way free. She begged them to make it stop, to release her, promising them anything if they let her free. Words flowed from her lips without meaning. Logan stroked her hair and whispered into her ear—soft, reassuring words that took the edge off.

The pain ebbed at last, and Kara forced her eyes open. A mass of dark shadow, like a tangle of small, slickened eels, hung in the air between her stomach and Salizar's hands. It moved, still alive. Energy pulsed along it every few seconds.

Sweat drenched Kara's body. Her flesh wasn't torn, but the skin of her stomach burned bright red where the tendrils used to be. Would it scar like that? She collapsed backwards into Logan's lap, letting the built up tension drain from her body.

Salizar caught the magic eater between his hands and stepped back from the table. It writhed like a fish drowning on air.

"Destroy it now," Logan said.

Salizar pulled one tendril away from the mass, and a hollow shriek filled the room. The tendril separated, and Salizar dropped it on the ground and crushed it beneath his boot. Then he whispered a word in that same arcane language and disappeared.

Logan lunged for the space he used to be.

Kara blinked, not entirely sure she was in her right mind. He was just gone, empty space where he'd once stood, and the magic eater with him.

"Fuck!" Logan yelled. He kicked a cupboard door, and the glass vials atop it teetered, some spilling over and releasing acrid fumes into the air.

He knelt and began sweeping the powders on the floor out of the way with his hands, gradually exposing a large transport rune that'd been carved into the workshop's stone floor.

"How bad is this?" Kara asked, her voice scraping against her throat.

"Well, he has your blood and an enormous dose of potent magic in the magic eater, and I wouldn't be surprised if this transport rune connects to a Sanguine hideout."

"So, very bad." Kara closed her eyes so the ceiling would stop wiggling. Weight pulled her down, plastering her to the table. She tried to lift a hand, and it wavered in the air before sinking back.

Logan cursed, then she was being lifted in powerful arms, and they were moving through the castle. He stuck to the servant's passages, but they passed several people, judging by the intakes of breath and the weight of their eyes following after them.

Kara nuzzled into his neck and breathed him in, eyes closed. She wanted to absorb the moment while she could.

Logan took her to his room and laid on her on the bed. She reached for him when he stepped away, but he returned with a warm, wet cloth and began washing the blood runes off her stomach, moving gently when he had to touch the tender red lines.

Kara couldn't stop shivering. Her throat was raw from screaming, and her entire body ached. She was completely drained.

Logan finished bathing her stomach and brushed a hand across her brow.

"In the future, Kara…I'd rather you take another than see you suffer like that again."

She pressed her head against him and pulled him down to the bed with her. His heat wrapped around her as he pulled her into his chest and tugged the blanket up over them.

"It wasn't about that. I was upset and tired of the curse controlling me. Someone else wouldn't have fixed the issue. You said you'd used the magic eater before. You understand."

He stroked her hair. "I didn't have anyone to guide me, though. This is my fault. I should have warned you about the magic eaters. Should have told you about the escort mission with the princess. I didn't want to think about what would happen if I didn't make it back in time, and it cost you."

"It's not your fault, Logan."

There was a knock on the door in a stilted pattern.

"Come in," Logan called.

Rahj stepped into the room and shut the door behind him. He was dressed like a noble in a forest green tailcoat and a cream vest. Rahj's eyes glanced over them together in the bed. "I saw your signal."

Logan kept his arm wrapped tight around her. "Scour Salizar's workshop and rooms for anything pointing towards his mission and affiliation. We'll meet tomorrow to discuss what you find."

Rahj nodded. "Kara," he said, tilting his head in acknowledgment. "Good to see you again."

Kara managed a weak smile.

()

When Kara woke, she was still weak, but she already felt markedly better than she had on the demon's drip. It was the first quality sleep she'd gotten since taking it. Logan was plastered around her, and she was over-warm from his body heat and the bedcovers. She tried to slide away, and his arms tightened, pulling her back in. She rolled over in his arms to face him and took him in.

The muscled expanse of his bare chest rose and fell softly with each breath, pure power leashed by the softness of slumber. The fire in the hearth cast a golden shadow over his face, softening his harsh jaw and dark stubble. She trailed a hand down his chest, tracing the lines of his muscles, and the evidence of his desire grew hard against her. Heat pooled low in her belly.

Logan's eyes slid open, and they glowed gold. They held the stare, and his cock flexed against her leg. Logan groaned and rolled away from her. "Don't look at me like that."

Kara hid her grin.

"Like what?"

"Like I could give you the world with my dick."

"Well, could you?"

Logan looked back at her, eyes molten. "I can certainly try."

Kara snorted. "How are you holding up?"

"I'm unbelievably horny. I wake up so fucking hard it feels like my dick is going to burst, having done everything imaginable to you in my dreams. I want to slaughter any man that looks at you. And masturbating only takes the edge off. So, fine. I'm doing fine. I've had several dreams of impaling Jon on my sword. No less than five."

Kara laughed. She crawled on top of him and skated down his abs, tickling the fine hairs there with her breath.

His muscles contracted, and his cock bobbed up beneath her, brushing against her cheek.

Logan grabbed her shoulders. "Kara, you don't have to do this."

She looked up into his eyes. "I want to."

"You're still recovering from yesterday."

Kara tilted her head to the right and ran her tongue along the crown of his cock, licking up the bead of moisture that leaked from his slit. "Are you going to tell me to stop?"

Logan's head fell back, and he clenched the sheets in his fists. The tendons in his neck were flexed taut.

Kara slid him into her mouth and sucked the head of his cock. His hips thrust up, sliding him deeper.

Logan groaned. "Mother Night, that feels good."

She took him deeper, relaxing her throat so she could fit as much of him as possible. She gripped his balls in one hand and rolled them gently between her fingers.

The muscles in his thighs clenched. He wrapped a hand in her hair and gently guided her, coaxing her up and down the length of him.

Kara circled him with her tongue as she sucked. His hand gripping tight in her hair with his dick in her mouth turned her on, making her eager for him. She ground herself on his hard thigh as pleasure built within her.

"Fuck. That's it."

His cock pulsed in her throat. He was close. She moved faster, her lips tighter, and his hips seized, thrusting wildly as he groaned her name. Hot seed coated her tongue, and she swallowed it, sucking down every last drop.

Kara cleaned him with her tongue and moved up his body. The glow slowly faded from his eyes. He pulled her up and started kissing her, his stubble scraping her lips and chin. Kara made herself pull back. Her skin still stung from his kisses and she was hot with need, but she wanted to take things slow. She'd shattered in his arms yesterday, and he'd been so protective and gentle when taking care of her with Salizar, but she was hesitant to dive fully back in. So much had happened in the last few days, and whenever she slowed down to think about everything that'd transpired, her chest tightened. She wasn't even sure if her keening would return this month or not now that the magic eater was gone.

"I need time," Kara said.

Logan nodded, and she rested against his chest as he stroked through her hair.

"Can I attend the meeting with the Stygians? I should be there." Kara expected him to argue with her, but he nodded in agreement.

"We'll go together."

( )

JON, Rahj, Athar, and Thomas sat around a circular table in the meeting room. Nerves danced in Kara's stomach as she followed Logan inside. Thomas's eyes were hard and flinty when they fell on her, settling there before shifting away. Kara slid into one of the empty chairs and avoided looking at him. This wasn't the setting she'd imagined meeting him again in. Logan sat down beside her.

Athar's gaze slid over her tousled hair, and he grunted. "Thank the mother you two are tuppin' again. He's been a right bastard the past month. Knew yall'd be back together, though. Recognized that look in his father's eye, too."

Kara's cheeks flushed, and she caught the small smile curling Logan's lips.

Logan cleared his throat. "Enough about my bedroom activities. Is the room secure?"

Rahj nodded. "Scanned and sealed."

"What's with all the rabble? Thought this was a circle meetin'." Athar said.

"Thomas is reporting to the other teams in the city, and the matter directly concerns Kara. What have you found?" Logan asked.

"There wasn't much—seems Salizar was vigilant about destroying evidence, but we found a letter." Rahj pulled a piece of parchment from his jacket and unfolded it. "Tricky piece of work, runescribed so that only a blood key would display the message. I was able to counter the lock eventually, but it's sophisticated. We're not dealing with amateurs." Rahj slid the paper across the table, and Kara and Logan read it together.

SHE WILL BE *in the palace soon. Inform me of her movements. Do no harm—we mean to take her alive.*

"THE PRINCESS," Kara concluded, sliding the letter back. "They mean to capture her, not kill her."

"More leverage. She's also the only heir aside from Calim," Jon said.

Kara kept her mouth shut. If Namirah was her grand-mother—and it was a big if—she wouldn't be in the line to succeed, anyway, having been born out of wedlock. And she had no interest in ruling this mess.

Rahj tapped his fingers against the table. "The tele-portation rune in Salizar's workshop—transporting objects is one thing, but people? I've never heard of it being done successfully. A friend of mine lost a hand attempting it, and he only teleported across his bedroom. I'd be surprised if he arrived on the other side intact. The magic singe on the rune was powerful, though. Whatever reagent he used to charge it was potent."

"Assume he made it," Logan said, his face tightening.

Kara's heart stuttered. Was he going to share the theory of her heritage with them? She wasn't ready to accept it herself, let alone share it with the world. Her heart swelled a little when he didn't elaborate.

Rahj arched a brow, his eyes ever-knowing. "So what's our next step?"

"Were you able to trace where the transport sent him?" Thomas asked.

Rahj shook his head.

"We have to assume Kara's cover is burnt," Jon said. "Salizar likely has runes all over the palace, which means he might have known her identity from the start."

"We need to continue the charade," Logan said. "It will keep us near the princess. Stay armed. If anyone attacks, they'll tip their hand. I'll have extra eyes on Kara and Ariana. Kara will take the news to Calim. It might be time to inform the princess of the threat, but I'll leave the decision to him."

"The Gavrochean delegation is arriving by ship this week," Rahj said. "The enemy will act soon if they want to stop the betrothal announcement."

Logan knit his fingers together. "Pull Jasper and Eric's squads in from the city, then. Put them wherever they'll fit—kitchens, courtiers, stableboys. I want everyone on this. Is there anything else?"

The room was silent.

"If you see something, say something. Snuff the seventh candle from the eastern entrance on the second floor servant's hall if you have information. We'll find you."

Everyone began to stand. Kara took a deep breath. "Thomas, may I speak with you? Alone."

His eyes flicked to hers, icy emotion warring within them. "I suppose."

Kara worried her thumb across her fingers as the others left the room. Maybe Thomas wouldn't try and kill her. She was still weak, and she didn't have any weapons with her.

He sat back down, crossed his arms across his chest, and propped his feet up on the table. "Well?"

Kara struggled to find the words she wanted to say. "I'm sorry for hurting you and betraying your trust. I know sorry isn't enough, and that I'll probably never warrant your trust or friendship again, but I want you to know I feel terrible about what I did to you. I was desperate, and it made me rash."

"You used me, Kara. I thought we were friends, but you manipulated me into divulging the location of the safe-house. Then you kept lying to me."

"I know. The prisoner was—*is*—my brother, the only family I know." Her eyes fell. "At least I thought I knew him. I hope you didn't suffer any lasting damage."

Thomas grunted. "Some bruises. I was more pissed that you took my glasses. Had to fumble around for a week waiting on the damn lenscrafter."

Kara winced. "I have them still. I always intended to return them. Eventually."

He snorted. "I haven't forgotten the favor you owe me."

"Just tell me what you need."

"I need out of this fucking palace. I'm sick of the ass-kissing and politics. And my itchy fucking uniform."

"Where do they have you stationed?"

"I ride around the city all day delivering messages. Jasper's been a right pain in the ass. Set his sights on me once you were gone."

Kara winced. "I don't expect you to forgive me immediately, for everything to go back to the way it was between us…but I'd like to work toward that."

Thomas nodded. "I'll try, but I can't promise you anything."

"That's all I can ask."

CHAPTER TEN

Kara took the information about Salizar's betrayal and suspected allegiance to Calim. He asked if there was any chance the mage had worked alone, without Sanguine influence. He also insisted they keep the danger a secret from Ariana still, not wanting to rock the boat before her betrothal announcement. Prince Rand was due at the capital any day now.

Kara wasn't entirely comfortable with his call—she'd prefer to know if someone was trying to have her killed or abducted—but she deferred to Calim's judgment. She was thankful when he let her escape without bringing up Namirah again.

Calim sent her a hefty sum of gold as a reward for identifying Salizar, despite his escape. In addition to the wages she'd already accrued, it was enough to run with and be comfortable for a long time—two years at least. She could escape Logan, the clan, everything. The attraction between them was destructive, and if she gave into it— embraced it fully—she might be lost forever. Part of her, the part that had exulted in him groaning beneath her with her tongue on his silken cock, wanted to abandon all hesitation—to crawl into his bed and make up for lost time.

Kara's eavesdropping runes were working now that the magic eater was out of her system, as she discovered one day when she saw a red glow coming from the depths of her armoire. The runes on her keystones lit up with a bloody red glow when they had a sound stored within. Kara listened to the stored messages regularly and began drawing more runes throughout the castle, determined to separate her feelings about Ariana from her duty to her. She had to be sneaky, as Serena and Rahj were in the process of locating and scrubbing all of Salizar's runes still. So far she'd gleaned much gossip and little of actual substance.

Her keening returned with a vengeance with the magic eater's absence, and she needed to figure out a solution other than stabbing Ariana over dinner soon. The princess still fawned over Logan, though now he largely ignored her and went out of his way to ensure Kara knew he was thinking of her, finding tiny moments to lock eyes, brush her thigh with his, or give her lingering touches that heated her blood. It reassured her and placated the beast inside her that hungered for blood, but she danced closer to that keening edge every day.

This morning in the courtyard, Jon had to pull her away from a skirmish after Kara drew Pippa's blood with a reckless blow. She felt terrible about it and apologized profusely, but Pippa looked at her with wary eyes afterward. The keening was making her heady, bloodthirsty. In her dreams, Logan took her in frenzied encounters in the palace hallways while people looked on. She exulted in their eyes watching. In proving they belonged to one another.

News of the Gavrochean delegation's ship anchoring

offshore reached the palace while they were still in the training yard, and they adjourned training early so everyone could prepare, though the princess looked none too pleased. Prince Rand was due to arrive tonight to much fanfare. A special ceremony would be held in the dining hall to welcome him to the palace and introduce him to Ariana.

When Kara entered the dining hall in the low cut ruby gown Merry had dressed her in that night, the setting had been transformed. Diaphanous red gauze hung over the multi-story windows. Candles littered the tables, lighting the room in a murky, sensuous glow.

Kara found a seat at a table with Pippa and Tanith, relieved to see the princess sat by Calim at the head of the main table. A man with olive skin and kind eyes sat at the princess's right, dressed in a golden silk tunic. Prince Rand, Kara presumed. Rand was far less decrepit than Ariana had led them to believe—he looked to be in his mid-thirties, and he had a handsome, regal bearing. Logan was across the room, but he found her immediately in the sea of people. She could feel the weight of his eyes on her.

The candles flickered, and drums began to play. A slow, seductive beat filled the room. The braziers in the corners started to smoke as the servants placed clusters of herbs atop the coals. The scent that floated throughout the room was subtle spice and smoke. Kara's eyes grew heavy. The gauzy curtains behind the stage musicians usually played on parted, and six dancers appeared. Four women and two men wound their way onto the stage, hips sliding to the beat. Jewelry dripped from them. Bracelets, necklaces. Rings for every finger and ears lined with gold. Some of them were studded with piercings in their noses, lips, navels, and clavicles. Each dancer was dedicated to a particular jewel. Diamond, sapphire, ruby, emerald, topaz, and amethyst were present. They wore a mix of loose, flowing pants and skirts split up to the waist that allowed flashes of their legs. Cropped tops bared their midriffs. Masks fashioned of strips of translucent fabric covered their eyes, dyed to match their chosen jewel.

"Do you think those jewels are real?" Tanith whispered to Pippa.

Pipes joined the steady drumbeat, and the dancers undulated like snakes. Their hips jerked in time with the music, taut bellies surging in and out, up and down. It was hypnotizing. Their jewels flashed in the candlelight.

The audience fidgeted in their seats, legs turned restless by the hazy energy captured in the room, straining at the edges to be released. Kara realized she was serpentining her hips in tiny circles beneath the table and rolling her shoulders softly.

Pippa leaned over, the warm crush of her dress and press of her toned body heating Kara's blood. Her mark warmed beneath her cuff.

"I've heard they burn a plant that acts as an aphrodisiac during these performances. Leaves people with fond memories of the evening, if you know what I mean. If you've got your eye on a particular lord, you should capitalize on it tonight."

Kara's mouth watered, and she swallowed her excess spit. *Fuck.* She had not come prepared for sex smoke.

The tempo of the music increased, and their dance became more frenetic. The dancers writhed. Their jewels shook. The drums pounded in her ears. A frenzied energy hung over the room like a wave about to break. Her mark itched, and the back of her neck was hot. The sapphire dancer's rippled abdomen gleamed with sweat, and Kara couldn't look away.

Logan's gaze on her felt like a live brand. She could smell his arousal drifting through the smoke. She twisted her head away from the dancers, and her eyes fell on him immediately, pulled there like an anchor. His eyes caught hers and trailed lazily down her body. His exploration missed nothing. It was slow, methodical. Utterly licentious. Kara's core pulsed.

The smoke in the air grew thicker. The drummers reached their peak. Kara stood up too fast, her silverware clattering on the table. She needed to get out—escape before she was nothing but a writhing, wanton mass on the floor. Kara fled the room, and Logan followed her like a dark promise.

CHAPTER ELEVEN

Kara exited the palace and sucked in deep breaths of fresh air, trying to clear her mind. But the air was muggy, her sweat sticky on her skin, and the erotic suggestions her mind supplied refused to fade. She could almost hear the drumbeat still thudding through her blood. She needed room to breathe, to think.

Kara fled towards the stables and searched for Drum. She found her in a stall next to the other Stygian horses. The stable attendants were absent; they likely snuck away to join in the festivities. She quickly saddled her mare and headed for the forest.

Kara rode deeper into the royal forest than she'd ever been before. Tonight it was not so menacing. Moonlight shattered the shadows, and her mind was too consumed by lust and thoughts of Logan's heated gaze to imagine what might lurk in the darkness. The intimate rocking of the saddle between her thighs taunted her. Her mark burned so hot her silver cuff stung her skin. She tore it off and shoved it into a saddlebag.

Kara rode deeper into the forest's depths, and its magic curled around her.

He's yours, dark seduction whispered in her ear. *Why do you run from him? He is your consort. He is strong, worthy. I have looked within his mind's scarred depths, and it is only for you.*

Kara shook her head, trying to block out the hot hum that buzzed across her skin. She came to a clearing beneath the limbs of a large tree and reined in Drum. Dense fog clung to this patch of forest. Fireflies skimmed along the moss gathered at the tree's roots. Moonlight filtered through the branches overhead, casting a shadow lattice on the ground that trembled in the wind.

This is a secret place, that strained, distant voice whispered.

Kara dismounted and looped the reins over the saddle horn so Drum could graze. She pulled the water flask on the saddle from its clasp and took a sip, hoping it held alcohol, but stale, warm water met her tongue. She paced, drank, paced some more, and when her bladder was full she itched all the more for it.

Kara circled the tree and stilled. The opposite side of the trunk hosted an altar stone stained with old blood. An antlered deer's skull hung behind it, nailed to the tree.

The wind blew and bones clattered. She jerked her head up. Animal skeletons littered the tree branches. They'd been carefully reconstructed, tied together at the joints, and hung here. A snake slithered in the wind. Birds bobbed up and down. A wolf was poised to bite, its incisors sharp and curved. Kara shuddered, and they mimicked her, dancing in the still air.

The soft snort of a horse alerted her to his arrival. She knew he was there, his presence as sure as the racing heartbeat in her chest. Hot breath billowed from Char's nostrils, clouding the air.

Logan dismounted and crossed to her, taking in the altar and the skeleton tree with a curious look.

"You'd rather fuck beneath the skeleton tree than in my bed?"

"Who said we were fucking?"

"You will, before this night is through."

Kara shivered at the promise in his words. "You know this place?"

"We both do."

Memory of her vision during her Stygian initiation flooded back, when she'd felt Logan press her to the altar stone and heard the tinkling of bones. She was always going to end up here. They were inevitable.

Kara gulped, her throat dry despite the water she'd guzzled. "You saw it too?"

Logan nodded. "Though I didn't believe it until now."

"Why did you follow me?"

"This forest is deadlier than the Blackshear. Namirah's magic lingers here, and someone could be following you. Don't worry. I won't do anything you don't ask me for."

Kara did not like the sound of that. She was weak where he was concerned.

He ran a hand over the altar stone, moving closer. "You didn't run very far. Maybe you wanted me to catch you."

"I wasn't running."

"You're always running, Kara."

She'd ran toward her destiny instead of escaping it. Heat squirmed between her thighs.

He moved closer, and she backed away. They pursued each other around the stone in a slow dance.

"I tried to stop this. The magic eater—it was all for nothing."

"That drug was a crutch, and you have forgotten the burn as it roars across your skin. I'm pleased you helped me with my keening already. Now I can take my time, make you beg." He held her gaze with feral yellow eyes, the heat banked in their depths promising carnal delights.

Inviting Logan back in, sleeping with him again, would mean he could hurt her. She was reluctant to relinquish that power, the safety of indifference. Not that she had ever managed indifference with him.

His eyes dipped down her chest, and he licked his lips. Kara followed his gaze, dismayed to find that she was halfway out of her dress, the sleeves and bodice hanging down from her waist, exposing her breasts and tight nipples. She had no recollection of undressing.

She stopped moving away from him, and Logan stilled.

"Strip and get on the altar," he said in a dark rumble.

Kara forced the dress down over her hips, ignoring the pop of stitches and buttons.

She slid onto the altar and crawled toward him on her knees. He was still fully clothed, his eyes hungry.

Logan curled his hand around the nape of her neck and started to massage. "Your skin is so hot. Your eyes liquid gold. I could drown in those eyes."

Kara wanted him to part her thighs and touch her, wanted him to loosen the control he always kept so tight. She was burning from the outside in.

He lay one cool gloved hand against her cheek, and she pressed into it like a cat, seeking relief from the flames licking at her skin. Sweat glistened on her brow.

He trailed a finger down her sweat-streaked abdomen. "You make a pretty sacrifice."

Kara spread her legs apart as his fingers went lower, silently begging him to touch her.

"You need this," he said, cupping her sex in his gloved hand and squeezing. The texture of smooth leather against the softest, most sensitive part of her was salacious, erotic.

She wanted him to part her lips and drag his finger across her clit. She started grinding against his hand, and he pulled away. She whined in her throat.

He tugged off his gloves and pulled his shirt overhead, muscles rippling along his skin. Then he slowly unlaced his leather bracers, baring himself to her fully, and let them fall to the ground. His mark glowed in the dark, and a thrill coursed through her. He bared himself for her, body and soul, stripping off the armor he wore for all others.

But rather than sate her need, Logan went back to teasing. His head fell to her breasts, and he tugged on her nipples with his teeth until they were taut and aching. He swiped one finger through her folds, purring in satisfaction when he felt how wet she was. Her nerves jangled at the brush against her hyper-sensitive clit. Then the infuriating man went back to smoothing his hands across her skin, massaging the space where her ass met her thighs with strong, deep fingers. He periodically stroked his thumb between her legs, letting tension coil inside her, then backed off as she neared release.

Kara thrashed, pressing herself into him. "Please," she groaned. "What do you want from me?" Her mark throbbed as insistently as her core.

"Ask me for it, Kara. Say you're mine."

He wanted her to admit defeat. She growled and gnashed her teeth. She dove a hand between her legs, determined to finish herself off if he was going to deny her. It would not solve the keening, but at least she would have some relief.

He caught her hand and pinned it above her head, his dangerous body stretched out over her. "Tonight is mine," he growled. "*You* are mine."

He slid back and traced his lips along the arches of her feet, her calves, her inner thighs, the patch of hair on her mound. Everywhere but where she needed them. She fell back against the stone, spread her legs as wide as she could, and drew her feet up to the edge of the altar, presenting for him. He blew air on her exposed clit, and she shuddered and bowed her hips towards him. Tears leaked down her cheeks, the skeletons dancing overhead blurring. Her nails dug into the unforgiving stone. She was mindless putty in his hands. "Logan," she moaned.

Logan pulled back and stood. He unlaced his breeches and pulled his stiff cock out, fisting his hand over it with quick jerks.

Kara sat up on her elbows and stared at him, at his swollen member, red and angry and leaking precum. He was not nearly so unaffected as he pretended to be. She wanted to yell at him to stop, to save all of it for her.

Logan wrapped his hands around her hips and jerked her to the edge of the altar. Her skin scraped against the stone's rough surface. Amber eyes stared into hers as he slid his cock between her inner lips, coating himself in her juices. He rubbed the swollen head against her clit. Kara's neck and back arched as sensation flooded her system, threatening to overwhelm her.

She forced her head up, staring down at the erotic portrait of him rocking against her, parting her soaking folds, threatening to slide home every time he thrust. Pleasure built. Kara neared her peak, muscles tightening as she rode the high. Just as she approached the edge, he pulled away with a curse.

"Goddess you drive me crazy." He was panting, his cock jerking in the air, as eager for release as she was.

Kara snarled in frustration. She attacked him, claiming his mouth and pulling him toward her. She bit his lip until she tasted blood. She gripped his slick cock and ran her hand from root to tip, milking it. It jumped in her hand.

He groaned and grabbed her hands, holding them captive against his chest. His eyes burned bright, his mark a deep red.

"Say it," he growled. "Say please." His demanding tone sent more pulses to her greedy core.

Kara stared at him, her entire body thrumming. His golden eyes burned with desire, with the promise of the pleasure only he could give. She tugged his hand to her mouth. The rough callous of his thumb brushed her lower lip. She drew his finger between her lips and sucked, her eyes half-lidded with lust. She could taste herself on his fingers.

She needed this more than life. "Please fuck me, Logan."

The control he'd be holding onto for a lifetime snapped. Logan buried his entire length inside her with one thrust. Kara instantly came, convulsing around him. Her pussy clenched at him, sucking him in. She dug her nails into his biceps as ecstasy flooded her. The moan he made was the sexiest thing she'd ever heard. The muscles in her thighs were still spasming as she began to come down, floating back to earth.

"Beautiful," he whispered in her ear. His teeth tugged at her earlobe and nipped her neck, sending her climbing all over again.

He pulled back, nestling his cockhead in the mouth of her pussy, circling there. Kara's hips surged against him. Then he sunk slowly into her clutching depth, and they both groaned.

"You're mine," he growled into her ear as he thrust in and out of her with rough pumps of his hips, claiming her body.

"I'm yours." She didn't know how many times she repeated it, mindless as he moved inside her, stretching her out with his large size. She wrapped her hands around his neck and her legs around his back as he fucked her on the edge of the altar. The wet slap of flesh filled the clearing. Logan gripped her hips hard enough to bruise, lost to sensation.

Kara fell back against the stone, abandoning herself to pleasure. Logan lifted her legs and hooked them over his shoulders, pushing the tops of her thighs to her chest as he leaned forward and plunged inside her. The position let him go even deeper, and he rubbed against a delicious spot inside her each time he thrust. His gaze went unfocused, his movements rougher as he neared climax.

He began rubbing small circles around her clit as he ravaged her, and fire climbed up her spine. Her back arched violently as another orgasm swept her, shuddering through her body. Possessed by something she didn't understand, Kara grabbed his wrist and bit into the skin of his mark until he bled. His whole body convulsed, his cock swelling as he spilled inside her, filling her up.

"Kara," he groaned, collapsing on top of her, hissing through his teeth when she adjusted her hips. He brushed a sweaty strand of her hair out of her face and gathered her in his arms. "That was…"

"I know." She was utterly spent. Drunk on pleasure. Floating on a cloud.

Logan slid his hands behind her back and lifted her against him, still inside her. He stood and carried her away from the stone. She winced as air hit her scraped thighs and back.

"Are you hurt?" There was a thread of dread in his voice.

Kara nuzzled into his neck and rested her head there, breathing him in. "I'm fine, Logan. Take me to your bed."

He rumbled his assent.

CHAPTER TWELVE

Kara awoke splayed on top of Logan. Each of his breaths raised her as his chest expanded and sank. Her skin was gross with dried sweat, and she was uncomfortably wet between her thighs. The night before came back to her slowly. Their passionate mating at the skeleton tree, then they'd dressed and ridden back to the castle, where they made love in his bed multiple times. They'd fallen asleep in post-coital bliss, and she hadn't had an opportunity to wash herself. The room reeked of sex. Her entire body ached. She was sore between her legs from their frenzied lovemaking, and scrapes from the stone altar littered her back and thighs. Even her mark was sore, and when she glanced at it, she saw it was lightly bruised with teeth marks.

She blushed to remember how she'd bitten him during her orgasm, discovering the delicious pain-pleasure response it triggered. When they returned to the palace, she'd begged Logan to bite her, to feast on her body, to pull her hair and fuck her with a hand tight on her throat. She'd ridden him, then he'd taken her from behind, clutching her ass as he filled her. They'd made love again and again, eager to make up for lost time.

Kara's hand crept to her throat, and she breathed a sigh of relief when she felt the familiar thong of the contraception charm. She'd forgotten all about it in their frenzy, had begged him to fill her with his seed multiple times. The memory of it sent tingles of sensation shooting towards her core.

She'd never been in a position to desire children. Researchers at the mage college claimed the curse wasn't genetic, but she worried about passing it on nonetheless. If she was truly of Namirah's line—though she still struggled to admit it—there could be an inherited element to her curse.

Logan's breathing changed, and when she glanced at him, his eyes were on her, tracing her face. "I was afraid you wouldn't be here when I woke up."

A pang went through Kara's chest. "I'm not going anywhere."

A sound of pleasure rumbled from his throat.

"How rough do I look?"

He frowned and flipped her over onto her back, diving for her neck and kissing and nibbling there. He moved along her jaw until he reached her lips. "You look," he said between kisses, "like a woman well-loved." He sniffed deeply and smiled. "Though we could both do with a bath. Good thing our room has a tub," he purred. "Our last encounter in one ended too soon."

Kara laughed and returned his kisses. "*Our* room?"

"I want you to stay with me."

Kara wished she could freeze this moment. Logan was so happy and carefree, hair mussed from lovemaking, the shadow that always followed him banished.

"But the ruse—"

"Is likely blown anyways. And I worry less about your safety if you're close by. I'll take Lady Grey off the marriage mart if I must. I've ruined her after all," he said, eyes dancing.

Kara stilled. "Are you serious?" How could he speak of marriage when they'd never even spoken of love? When she was still outcast from the clan? Surely he meant a fake engagement of sorts—another layer for the disguise.

"Deadly."

Kara tried to stuff down her disappointment. "Merry is going to be very confused. She thinks my heart's for Viscount Kendrick."

A menacing growl rolled from Logan's chest. "I don't like the way he looks at you."

Kara rolled her eyes. "You really are an animal."

"Like attracts like."

"He's Jasper's brother, you know."

"All the more reason not to like him. Now, enough talk of Kendrick. I believe you and I have an appointment."

Kara squealed as Logan swept her into his arms and rose from the bed, heading for the bath.

()

KARA RETURNED to her room to gather the essentials she'd need if she was staying with Logan. When she opened the armoire, there was a red glow coming from its depths. Kara dug through her pile of keystones for the glowing one, pushing aside skirts and random items she'd chucked in there.

The rune on the stone glowed a bright red. It was one from the library, according to her labeling. Kara pricked her finger with her dagger and touched her blood to the rune.

The first sounds that came out of the rock were rustling skirts and a breathy moan.

"Not here," a feminine voice said. "Someone might see."

There was a male chuckle and the creak of a door.

Kara smiled. She'd yet to see anyone use the library for reading besides Calim.

The runestone pulsed, and a new recording began playing. It featured a maid humming a tune to herself as she cleaned.

Kara was losing hope of hearing anything useful when the third recording began.

"Prince Rand. I didn't expect to find you here."

Kara stilled when she recognized Ariana's voice.

"I'd like to spend some time with you, princess. Get to know one another. We're due to be wed, but you've been avoiding me since I arrived. Am I not to your liking?"

"My brother hasn't told you, has he?"

"Told me what?"

"He's changed his mind. He won't be announcing any betrothal. I assumed you wouldn't want to see me after such news—"

"I saw the king this morning, and he said nothing of it."

"I apologize. This isn't news he should keep to himself, now that he's decided. Some people just aren't meant to lead."

"But the trade deal—they spent months on this—we sailed for *weeks*. Is he mad? I will speak to the king myself."

"Let me know if you find him. I've been searching all day myself. Probably holed up somewhere, pining."

The red glow faded. Kara frowned and slid the stone into her pocket. Why would Calim cancel the betrothal? Had Ariana made up her mind about Rand already and convinced Calim to reconsider? Was it all a ruse on her part?

When Kara returned to Logan's room, he was propped up in bed reading, sheet gathered around his hips. She licked her lips as she imagined dragging the sheet off him and crawling up his body. She set her things down and slid into bed with the grimoire.

"What've you got there?"

"The grimoire Salizar gave me. I thought it might contain some clues."

Logan stiffened beside her. "You've been practicing blood magic? With him?"

"Not *with* him, per se. He didn't show me much. But I've been studying the book. He did say something odd…" Kara flipped the book open to a page with marginalia and turned it to Logan. "Can you see this writing on the edges here? By my finger?"

Logan looked at the page, then glanced up at her face and shook his head. "There's nothing there."

Kara's mouth went dry. "Fuck. Salizar said the same thing. Claimed he found it in the palace. The book is full of custom runes and advice for their uses."

"Maybe he spelled it so only you could see? The custom runes could be a trick."

"I don't think so. Their forms make intuitive sense, and the variations I've tried have worked. I think it might have belonged to Namirah."

Logan pulled her into his arms and kissed her brow. "Promise me you'll be careful."

"Sometimes I think I hear her…whispering to me. Like at Widow's Fall, or at the altar in the royal forest."

Logan's eyes flashed amber at the mention of the altar. "Is it out loud? Or in your head?"

"I don't know," Kara admitted.

"And what does she say?"

"Advice, oddly enough."

Logan pursed his lips and swallowed.

"You think it's true that she's my grandmother."

"I don't believe in coincidences, Kara. Especially this many. Is it not better, in the end, to know? Or were you more content before?"

Kara rested her head against his chest and listened to the steady beat of his heart. "I'm not sure. I still know nothing about my mother and father. And Namirah's so infamous… I don't know what would happen if people found out we were connected. Childhood was hell enough."

Logan stroked his fingers over the back of her head. "I love you just the same."

Kara's heart stuttered.

"What did you say?"

"I said I love you, Kara McKenna. Cursed or not, Namirah's granddaughter or not—I love *you*."

Kara froze. "You do?" This was the last thing she'd expected.

Her chest burst with emotion. She ought to respond, to confess that she loved him, too, but she was overwhelmed. How could she encapsulate how she felt about him into three little words? They were so insufficient.

"Logan—"

"I know, Kara. There need be no words between us."

She turned her face up to his and lost herself in him.

CHAPTER THIRTEEN

Kara woke to a gloved hand wrapped around her mouth. Her heart stuttered into awareness, and she swung her eyes around the room, blinking rapidly to clear her vision. People in head-to-toe black encircled the bed, leaning over her and Logan, and someone across the room chanted in a low voice. The tip of a knife poked into her throat,

Kara's eyes swung to Logan. He was still asleep, his arms cradled beneath the pillow and face turned towards her. A stranger with a knife poised over Logan's back put a finger to their lips.

Kara's chest tightened. Why wasn't Logan waking? His senses were usually otherworldly.

The man at the end of the bed jerked his head, motioning for her to get up. Adrenaline throttled her sleep addled brain. Whoever they were, if they wanted her dead, they'd have killed her already. She took the gamble.

Kara bit into the gloved hand over her mouth, and the man let out a string of curses. She snapped her hand toward the dagger at her throat as she kicked Logan, trying to wake him.

Logan's shoulders twitched, his head raising off the pillow before sinking back down.

"Logan!" Kara screamed as she grappled with the man for his knife, trying to keep it away from her flesh.

But no sound came from her throat. She tried screaming again, her throat ripping with the effort, and she was met with silence. Logan's shoulders began to shake.

"I thought you said he was out!" a masked female said.

"He should be!"

"Give him more!" the female said.

One of Logan's eyes slid open, revealing a pupil ringed with red.

"Plan B!"

The dagger plunged into Logan's shoulder. He roared as he sprang off the bed. Another stab, this time catching him in the arm.

Kara faltered, distracted, and the man she tussled with caught her arms and twisted them behind her back.

A cluster of attackers circled Logan, closing in on him. Kara's stomach plummeted as dark red lines ran down his naked body.

Logan snapped out a kick, and one of the assailants screamed as his shin crumpled beneath him. Another one was thrown into the dresser, and the wood cracked beneath their back. Logan was staggering through his motions like a bear woken early from hibernation, so unlike his usual lithe and deadly movements.

Kara's eyes darted to the robed figure in the corner, still chanting under his breath. She reared her head back, snapping her skull against the face of the man caging her arms, then rushed the mage.

The mage reached a hand into a pouch on his belt,

raised his palm to his lips, and blew. A puff of purple powder clouded the air, covering her face. It crawled up her nostrils and choked her throat. She had the awful sensation of dust in her eyes, but her eyelids refused to close when she tried to squinch them shut.

Then her limbs froze, her arm still outstretched toward him. Her legs refused to move. Her mouth froze in a gasp. Her body began to tilt forward, a statue pushed off balance. Her outstretched arm took the brunt of the fall as she crashed to the ground. Her eyes slowly swept around their sockets, crazed, looking for Logan.

Kara watched, paralyzed, as more flashing daggers sunk into his flesh. Logan's blood spattered her face with a wet slap. His attackers swarmed him, hanging onto his limbs as he thrashed and tried to shake them off. He fought them with everything he had, but he was suffering the mage's spell and vastly outnumbered. He sank to the floor, chest covered in blood, and twisted his head towards her. She'd only seen Logan looked scared a handful of times. After her fight with Cervus, when she was dying and he'd used the sanguinata to save her. When he'd discovered the demon drip's dark mark crawling across her stomach. And now. Pain and fear lit his eyes as he bled out, losing strength.

Kara railed against her body, willing herself to move, to ignore the paralytic. Then the mage knelt over her, blocking her view of Logan. Pale green eyes shined over his mask. *Salizar.* She was going to make him wish he'd never been born.

Salizar touched the back of her head, and darkness embraced her.

()

WHEN KARA CAME TO, she was being dragged. Rough arms hooked beneath her armpits, and her legs slid behind her on the floor. She tried to blink, and her eyes slid shut slowly. The powder was wearing off. The hum of magic that buzzed across her skin was suffocating yet familiar. A harsh rattle accompanied her breath.

They dragged her down a long white hall in the palace that ended at a black door. Her captors slid the door open, revealing a lavish chamber. Ariana sat in front of her vanity, a monstrous piece of carved alabaster with a hulking mirror propped atop it.

Kara's eyes widened, her heartbeat speeding up. She tried to call out, to warn her, but the muting spell was still in effect.

The princess turned as the door shut behind Kara and her captors. Four men escorted her—the princess didn't stand a chance. Where were her guards? The Vespertines?

Ariana's expression didn't change as she took in the scene. Kara's mind screeched.

The princess rose from her padded seat and walked towards Kara, skirts swishing between her legs. "I've been looking into your history, Lady Grey. It doesn't exist. Who are you? One of my men paid old Lord Grey a visit. He was eager to talk once I waived his debt to the crown. Imagine my surprise when he said he has no children. He was shocked to learn he had a daughter at court, seeing as he's been sterile since the Curse Wars."

Kara mouthed silent words, trying to communicate. Were these Ariana's men? Why had Salizar been with them, and why had they attacked Logan?

"How long till the spell wears off?" Ariana snapped.

The man to Kara's right shrugged. "He didn't say."

"I will let you speak, but if you scream, your friends will suffer. Understand?"

Kara nodded, her mind still reeling. What friends did she refer to? Logan? The other Stygians? She needed to know if he was okay—there'd been so much blood, so many knives. They should have told Ariana about the threat—she'd gotten suspicious on her own, jumped to conclusions and taken action. Kara would be lucky if she survived this.

Ariana wet her finger with her tongue and scrubbed it across the nape of Kara's neck. The magic wrapped around her throat bubbled away, and Kara could breathe freely again.

"I mean you no harm, princess." Her voice came out sludgy and thick, still tainted by the magic.

Ariana gripped Kara's jaw and ran the long, sharp fingernail of her thumb down it. "Shall I tell you what gave you away?" Her nail pressed into the flesh of Kara's cheek. "The way you looked at him. No aristocrat would lust after a mongrel like Logan Vakarian so publicly. A dirty mercenary with a title bought with blood? Fine to fuck in the shadows, of course. But nothing real. Teleria has forgotten, though. She grows fat with complacency as the clans get stronger and the crown weaker. Something had to be done."

"I know I lied, but your brother hired me to protect you. I have your best interests at heart. Where's Logan? He was hurt—he needs medical attention."

Ariana cackled, her pristine face contorting in glee. "You still haven't figured it out? Goddess, you're a terrible spy. You should really consider another profession. Oh, wait—this one will be your last."

Kara stilled. They'd misread all the threats. Ariana had never been in danger, Calim had. *From Ariana. Fuck.* Did Calim even have anyone guarding him, or had he diverted everyone to guard his sister?

Ariana wrapped a curl of hair around her finger tight enough to turn the skin white. "You have no idea what you are, do you? What you will wreak on this world? All that precious power. What a waste. It has been amusing, watching you all stumble around, always a step behind. I'll miss it. It's too bad I promised you to Victus."

Ariana had allied herself with the Sanguines. Kara tried to quell the panic coursing through her. "Please, Ariana. You don't have to do this. Victus only serves himself. I don't know what he promised you, but you're only giving him more power. He won't help you win the crown."

"Take her," Ariana said with a wave of her hand. "And keep her unconscious. If she doesn't make it to Victus, you'll have the queen to answer to."

"What have you done to Calim, you traitor?" Kara spit, and the glob landed under Ariana's eye. The princess wiped it away with one long nail and flung it to the ground, leveling her gaze on Kara.

"Teleria is done with false kings. You and your lover will be charged with treason—an attempt by the Stygians to usurp the crown, thwarted by the Sanguines and I. But I'm afraid you'll miss the trial. You're going on a trip."

Someone pulled a black sack over Kara's head and yanked the strings tight against her throat. More hands set to binding her wrists and ankles. Kara screamed and kicked at them, writhing to try and escape. Someone lifted the back of the sack and painted something wet on the skin of her neck. That familiar magic bubbled back up, squeezing her throat and tongue, and silent darkness stole her.

()

KARA AWOKE TO DARKNESS. Crud pasted her eyelids together, and when she tried to draw a hand to her face, she met resistance. Wide cuffs bolted her wrists to the wall above her. She tried to move her feet, and the sharp sting of raw ankle skin against metal confirmed her fears. Her legs were spread, cuffs securing them against the wall. She tilted her neck, stretching it, and the raw ache that slithered down her shoulders elicited a gasp.

The thin shift she'd worn to bed last night stuck to her thighs with sweat. Her head was pounding with the after-effects of trauma, dehydration, and Salizar's spells and powders. She licked her chapped lips, and her mouth split at the inner corners. She waited in silence, wishing oblivion would pull her back under. Something hairy darted across her bare foot, and she bit her lip to keep from screaming. Hopefully the rats were well fed.

The scent of cloistered damp and stale piss curled up her nose as her senses woke from their stupor. The details of the night before crept back. Ariana, blue eyes burning in victory. She hoped Calim was watching his back. Serena, too. Memory of Logan exploding in fury until blood washed down his chest played through her head. She clenched her eyes shut and took a deep, wet breath. He was alive—he had to be. Her brain refused to entertain the alternative. She whispered her name into the dark, relieved when it creaked out. The silencing spell had worn off.

A corona of yellow light bloomed in the distance, details of her surroundings becoming clear as it bobbed towards her. Dark stone walls and metal bars lined the corridor. Her cell was at the very end, facing the interminable hallway.

Footsteps neared, heavy and confident. Their owner slowed in front of the cell, face washed out by the bloom of light. Kara went limp and closed her eyes, pretending at unconsciousness. Hopefully it would spare her examination and questioning or allow her to get the jump on them. A key jostled in the lock, and the door swung open on creaking hinges.

The light glowed behind her eyelids as her jailer stepped close. They smelled of woodsmoke and wine. Strong fingers gripped her jaw and lifted her face. A thumb caressed the curve of her cheek, down her jaw to her neck.

"Now now, Kara. I've enough experience at this to know when someone is faking. It's all in the breathing. The heartbeat."

Kara opened her eyes. The light blinded her at first, his form slowly coming into view as her eyes adjusted.

A tall man with ash blond hair and stunning features stood beside a floating fae lantern. Dark brows swept over pale grey eyes and chiseled lips. He wore a collared white shirt under a red vest embroidered with the Sanguine sigil —roses wrapped in thorns. His shirtsleeves were rolled up to his elbows, exposing pale forearms corded with muscle.

"It's unfortunate we have to meet like this. I was hoping it'd be much more civilized, but Ariana is an impatient creature."

"Who are you?" Kara asked. It came out in a strained croak.

"My name is Victus. You might have heard of me."

Kara stilled. The leader of the Sanguines. *Fuck.*

Victus reached for his belt and lifted a flask to her lips. "Drink. It's water."

The metal rim was cold against her over-warm skin. Kara was hesitant to imbibe anything he offered, but she wouldn't last long without water. She fastened her lips around the flask, and he tilted it up, flooding her mouth. She guzzled it down as fast as she could, desperately lapping at the trails that fell down her chin when he pulled the flask away.

He watched her desperation with a keen, analyzing gaze. "You're out of sorts still from the pause powder. Nasty stuff. Ridiculous a team of ten required it. I regret not coming for you myself. Then again, they didn't expect to find you in bed with Vakarian. I thought you were through with him."

Panic tattooed her heart. "Where is he? Is he alive?"

Victus smiled, revealing unnaturally white teeth. "He's here. For now. How long he survives remains to be seen. Your cooperation could go a long way towards that."

"Prove it." He could be lying about Logan, using the threat as leverage. *He could also be lying about him being alive*, an insidious voice in her head whispered. There'd been so much blood.

"You'll hear evidence soon enough. My mages have never had an adult male Namirahn to toy with before. I doubt they will take it easy on him."

Kara surged forward against her bonds, pain shooting through her where raw flesh cut into metal. Her struggle was pointless.

Victus started laughing. "Don't suffer at your own hands, my dear. We'll accommodate you plenty in that regard."

"What do you want?"

"I've been looking for you for a very long time. You are the crown on my pyramid of jewels. It's a pity he's already tainted you." He traced the curve beneath her breast, where the thin shift molded to her body. "When was your last keening?"

"None of your fucking business."

Victus smiled, then he snatched a handful of hair and

yanked her head forward, his voice darkening. "I want answers and cooperation, or you will suffer, girl."

"I'll kill you for this."

"Hah. Logan, maybe. But you? How many keenings have you seen? Five? Namirah's progeny or not, you're an untested brat compared to me. Your lover's in chains. You betrayed your clan. I own your brother. No one is coming for you, and they couldn't find you if they tried. You have no one, Kara. I am your god. Prepare to bow down and pray."

How did he know about the link between her and Namirah? Had Salizar suspected and told him?

"Now, let me explain how this is going to work. You tell me what I want to know, and I won't hurt you. Much."

"What's your question?" she spat.

"To begin with, who is guarding Raven's Rest, with the Stygians in the east embroiled with the royals? How many?"

Kara looked into his clear eyes and smiled. Then she reared back and smashed her head into his face. It hurt him more than it hurt her. Victus cursed and stepped back, hand flying to his broken and bleeding nose. It'd been so straight before, too.

His eyes flashed. "There it is. That fire. I was beginning to wonder what Vakarian saw in you." He raised a hand to his face and popped his nose back into place with a grunt and a sickening crunch.

He smiled through the blood staining his teeth and left the cell. The fey lantern bobbed behind him, leaving her in darkness once more.

When the light disappeared, Kara called out into the darkness. "Logan? Are you there? Is anyone there?"

Silence answered. Kara rested her head against the damp wall, shifting in a fruitless attempt to rest as much of her weight as possible. Her arms were on fire from being stretched overhead for hours. She'd lost feeling in the tips of her fingers. She stretched and rotated her wrists, trying to wake up the blood flow.

She probably shouldn't have antagonized Victus—should've tried to stay on his good side for as long as possible. But he'd been after her since Mudbottom—always trying to capture, not kill. The other marked women he took were also held prisoner if they didn't come willingly. Whatever he wanted with her, he needed her alive to accomplish.

()

KARA EXPECTED Victus to return the next day, but he left her alone in darkness. One day bled into the next, her internal clock losing precision without the sun to guide her. The rats were her only companions, and they were growing bolder by the day, pausing to sniff at her toes instead of scurrying away when they brushed against her. She began to regret attacking Victus when no food or water came. She soiled herself when her bladder filled to bursting, warm urine trickling down her leg into her raw ankles. Luckily, her bowels hadn't moved—she hadn't eaten in days, and her body was shutting down those functions.

She was exhausted from standing. The skin of her wrists was so angry and raw that she feared it would just slide from her bones, shucked off from holding up the weight of her body. She fantasized about summoning a cloud she could float into the sky and lay on for eternity, never having to stand again.

Kara daydreamed about rescue. She thought she heard familiar voices in the distance. Logan's low growl, Jon's laugh. She would count out seconds into hours, telling herself that when she opened her eyes, salvation would be there.

So when the light at the end of the tunnel appeared again, Kara thought she was imagining it. Her heart sank when Victus's white blond head bowed in front of the cell door to unlock it. His nose was a mash of purple and green, though the bone had been set straight once more. Something unnerved her about the cut of his jaw, the way his muscles sat on his frame as he moved. They were all slightly familiar.

Victus stepped into the cell and set a bucket on the floor. "This all could have been avoided, you know. I should have killed Dondar when he ruined our ambush in Mudbottom."

One-Eye. Kara had already fulfilled his wish. Victus was wearing black today—was it because he expected to get blood on him?

"I'm going to let you down from the cuffs. If you fight, we will repeat the last three days again. I know how close to the brink I can push the Namirahn body, and you have only just glimpsed the edge. Do you understand?"

Kara nodded weakly. She was desperate for relief, even at Victus's hands.

He stepped forward and unlocked the ankle cuffs, and Kara groaned as the choking metal snapped free. Her skin blazed at the release of pressure from her inflamed flesh. Then her first wrist cuff creaked open, and her arm fell to her side with a dull thud. When the second cuff opened, Kara slumped forward, arms numb and body too exhausted to keep herself upright. Victus caught her against him, wrapping his arms around her.

In the back of her mind, Kara knew she should feel for weapons on Victus's person, should take advantage of this chance, but her body refused to follow her commands. Victus took on more of her weight as she slumped forward, unable to support herself. He lowered them to the ground together, folding her into his lap and resting her head in the crook of his neck.

Kara hated this mockery of compassion, but she was utterly spent. Victus held a waterskin to her lips and supported her head while she drank, her neck too tired to even hold her head up. She drank greedily, and he pulled the water away.

"Slowly, or you'll puke. Your stomach is weak."

Victus followed the water with a bowl of plain rice and shredded chicken that he spoonfed her. Then he removed a tin of white paste from his pocket and rubbed it into her ragged wrists and ankles. The contact burned like fire, and she grit her teeth against the pain, but she didn't resist. She was too weak to fight.

"It will not ease the pain or make you heal faster, but it will prevent infection."

Kara was beginning to see how Victus's captives might choose to side with him over lingering in his dungeons. He was a master manipulator. Is this what had happened to Wesley? Was he here? Hope swelled in her at the thought, but it was a fool's hope—she couldn't count on Wesley's aid. He'd proved he couldn't be trusted.

When she finished eating, Victus left the cell without chaining her back up. Kara embraced the moldering floor like it was a fine feather bed.

AFTER SLEEPING DEEPLY for the first time since she'd been captured and regaining a little of her strength, Kara explored her cell as best she could in the dark. She traced her fingertips along the wall, searching for loose stones or etchings from prisoners past. She discovered what felt like a cranking apparatus attached to a wheel, but when she tried to turn it, it caught and refused to budge.

Kara moved to the cell door and analyzed the lock. She didn't have anything to pick it with, but she could try a blood rune. Escaping the Sanguine stronghold alone while unarmed would be virtually impossible, but maybe she could find Logan. Assuming this was the hidden prison the Stygians and Saphia had been searching for—where Victus kept the women he'd taken—it didn't bode well for their chances of rescue. Even Rahj's spies had been unable to locate it. She was alone on her cell block, so if her suspicions were correct, there'd be other halls just like this one full of captives.

Kara scraped her finger against a sharp edge of the stone wall until blood welled, then traced an unlocking rune onto the cell door. Nothing happened. No click or pop of release, no dull glow of the rune. Kara tested the door, unsurprised when it didn't budge. The whole cell was probably warded against magic use, if not the entire prison. She sighed and rubbed away the rune with the precious little spit she had.

VICTUS RETURNED THE NEXT DAY. His usually mannered hair was tousled, and a long cut scabbed over with blood marred his cheek. Someone had gotten to him.

The cell clinked open, and Kara's eyes fell to his hands. He held two large silver hooks. They reminded her of meat hooks, the kind butchers hung animal carcasses with when bleeding them dry.

Kara scrambled backwards as he stepped close, putting her back flush with the wall. She'd been a fool to think him capable of compassion after yesterday. She was still so weak—too weak to fight him and hope to win.

"You're looking better today. I hope you're prepared to answer my questions." He slid the hooks against each other in a metallic shuffle.

Kara swallowed.

"Now, how many people are defending Raven's Rest? I've already sent my spies there; I have my suspicions. All you have to do is confirm it."

"I don't know anything of value, I swear. They kicked me out after I helped Wesley in Travincal."

"Ah, your brother. Or the sham of one, anyway. He has proven most loyal. I could arrange for him to visit you if you tell me what I want. Would you like that?"

Kara didn't speak.

"Shall we try another question? Who within the clan has magical abilities? How many?"

"You're wasting your breath and your time."

Victus tsked, crouching in front of her and running a hand down her face. "It doesn't have to be like this, you know. If you cooperated, I'd treat you like the princess you are. Take you above ground, give you a room and a bed and food from my table. Choosing survival isn't weak. Give me *something*."

Kara had been wracking her brain for information she might reveal that wouldn't hurt anyone, but everything revealed a weakness, made someone vulnerable. She could lie, but he might be testing her by confirming things his spies had already reported. She wouldn't be surprised if there were Stygians already in his pocket.

"I slept in the broken tower."

Victus sighed like a man who'd discovered his tea was improperly prepared. "Such a martyr. Who are you trying to protect? Your lover's already doomed, the rest of them forsook you. And here I thought you smart."

"Do what you will."

"Very well. Stand up and turn and face the wall. You might want to brace yourself."

Kara looked from the hooks in his hand to his face. They were wicked sharp on one end, the other side tipped with a metal ring.

"Please." She tried to slide away, but Victus blocked her with his arm and a slow shake of his head.

She ought to attack him, ought to explode in a flurry of violence, damn the consequences, but all the fight had gone out of her. Even if she bested Victus in her weakened state, who knew how many Sanguines awaited her upstairs? Fighting seemed pointless.

Kara turned around and clenched the wall, digging her fingers into the edge of an exposed stone.

Cold metal slid down her back, and a shiver rippled across her skin.

"Your skin will stretch. Fight me, and I'll put them through muscle."

Kara screwed her eyes shut, anticipating the pain. Victus pulled the skin above her shoulder blades up away from the muscle, stretching it taut. Then he shoved the hook through her skin with a quick motion. It burned, but it wasn't as bad as Kara had expected. He placed the second hook to the right of the first, punching it through the skin in a practiced motion.

Victus tugged on the hooks, and Kara gasped. He led her to the center of the room and removed two metal spheres spiked with curved barbs from his pocket. Kara blanched when he began screwing them onto the sharp end of the hooks. "Can't have you sliding off, slippery as you are."

Kara shivered and wrapped her arms around herself. She wasn't sure how she was going to get out of this one.

Victus unlocked the crank she'd found the night before and began to turn it. Two thick silver chains rattled as they descended from the ceiling.

Kara's stomach dropped when she realized what he planned.

"You're sick." She scoured the room for anything she could use as a weapon. She tried to reach behind her back for the barbs and twist them off so she could remove a hook, but they were out of reach of her arms.

"The more you fight me now, the longer you'll hang."

Kara closed her eyes and took a step forward.

Victus clipped the chains to the hooks in her back, the metallic snap echoing throughout the cell. Then he walked to the crank and began to turn.

Kara kept her toes on the ground as long as possible as the chains lifted, but eventually she was forced into the air. The tug of her full bodyweight against the hooks was uncomfortable, a constant dull pain rather than a sharp one. Victus pushed her hip, and she began to sway. The sawing of the hooks through the raw puncture holes made her want to scream.

"Right now you think you will get through this, that the pain is temporary. But do not mistake yourself. I will break you. The hooks make everyone sing eventually. It's exciting for me when they resist, endure. I so rarely get to the next phase. Think on your reticence a while." Then Victus left, the cell descending into darkness once more.

Kara's body dangled from the prison rafters—a grotesque mirage swaying in concentric circles. She gripped the chains and pulled herself up, willing her body to still. The motion took some of the pressure off her skin, but eventually her arms burned and shook until they gave out, and she collapsed back down onto the hooks. The pain was insidious. Dull at first, it spread into a relentless fire that arched across her back.

She knew the hooks only pierced her skin, but the longer they were in, the deeper they felt. Like they scraped against bone and meat. She imagined them ripping the muscle out from beneath her skin, but she'd still be caught there, hanging like some twisted marionette.

Kara didn't know how much more of this she could stand. When the pain spiked, she began to bargain with herself about what details she could tell Victus that would do minimal harm. Tried to convince herself it was okay to break. Then she'd become angry at her weakness and redirect her thoughts to embedding a hook in one of Victus's eyes and pulling it out the other.

One fevered sleep later, someone walked down the prison hallway. They carried no light, and their steps were lighter than Victus's, but that was all Kara could tell in the darkness. The figure stopped in front of the cell door and stared at her.

"Help," Kara pleaded.

The stranger turned and left without a word.

◯

Two sleeps later, the silent watcher came again. Kara was barely conscious, her body shutting down. She hardly recognized pain as a distinct sensation anymore—it was omnipresent. A key twisted in the lock, clicking the latch open, then the figure turned and left.

Kara's ears strained as footsteps disappeared down the hallway. Had she imagined the lock clicking open? Was it a trap, meant to punish her more if she tried to escape?

Kara counted out an hour, waiting to see if the

stranger or anyone else appeared, and then she kicked her legs forward, setting her body swaying. Her hooked skin was stretched thin already. She had two choices—try to pull the hooks out, barbs intact, or split the skin securing them. The latter seemed faster and less painful overall, though it was going to hurt like the mother regardless.

The chains swung through the air. Pain flared bright and hot as her abused skin stretched and tore. She clenched her teeth so hard her jaw ached and kicked through the air again. Then she gripped the chains and yanked them away from her with all her might.

Her skin ripped.

Kara couldn't hold in her scream.

She fell, knees crashing into stone. She sucked in a jagged breath. Then another. She could control this pain—wrap it in her mind's fist and squeeze until it snuffed out. Several heaving, gasping inhales later, Kara unscrewed her eyes.

She slowly climbed to her feet and unclipped the bloody hooks from the chains. Her back was a mass of throbbing, pulsing pain. Warm blood trickled down her back to her legs.

Kara made her way to the cell door and tested it, relief sinking through her when it swung open. She'd half expected it to all be for naught, that she'd imagined the stranger freeing her. Her heart raced as she dashed down the dark hallway on unsteady feet, feeling her way along the stone walls. She didn't know what awaited her at the end—it'd always been obscured by darkness or the halo of Victus's lantern.

She found a metal ladder embedded in the wall of a circular alcove at the end of the tunnel. A ladder to nowhere, into the abyss. Kara climbed until her head bumped against a solid surface. She pushed up, praying it wasn't locked, and the wooden hatch lifted.

Kara climbed out into another hall of cells that mirrored her own, but this one was dimly lit with fiery sconces. An endless supply of pain echoed through this level of the prison—sobbing and moaning, screaming, crazed grunts. The noise sent an uneasy current through her gut. Kara lowered the hatch behind her and glanced down at herself. Her skin was bruised and dirty, and there were bright stripes of raw flesh at her wrists and ankles. Her belly was concave beneath her bloody shift, and her mark had faded, its usual glow so dull it more closely resembled rusty blood. She needed a disguise if she was going to get anywhere, though the thought of tugging on a shirt over her torn back made her want to retch.

She swayed lightly on her feet, then gripped the hooks tighter in her hands and tried to get her bearings. There was no end in sight to the hallway in either direction. Kara chose left. She peeked into the cells she passed as she stumbled down the hall.

There was at least one woman in every cell. Some cuffed or chained to the wall, some suspended like Kara had been. Others were free, but they sat in the middle of their cells, staring into nothing. Several of them bore the dark star of a magic eater on their flesh, though none so large as Kara's had been. As Kara neared the end of the hall, a woman threw herself against her cell door.

"You're one of us! Help me. Get me out of here."

Kara glanced at the lock, then down to the hooks in her hands. She had no way to pick the lock, was in terrible shape herself. She had to keep moving. This floor was almost certainly warded against blood runes, too, given Namirahn powers. "I'll come back for you."

The woman laughed, and it was stretched and crazed. "No one comes back."

The last cell on the block held a woman shackled to a wall—they'd gone so far as to close a metal cuff around her neck, the first of those she had seen. Kara stilled. Dirty, knotted white blond hair half-covered a familiar face.

"Saphia?" she whispered.

The woman could barely turn her head. She blinked at Kara, exposing one clear eye and one purple with bruising, the white of her eye full of blood. Kara blanched when she saw the dark star of the magic eater crawling up the side of Saphia's cheek. Someone had put it there intentionally —every other prisoner she'd seen bore it on their arm, abdomen, or thigh.

Saphia opened her mouth to speak, then wet her lips and tried again. Her top lip was swollen and split. Kara's heart ached for her—for all of them.

"Keep. Moving." Her voice was a rasp. A whisper. She was barely hanging on. It'd been months since Travincal, when Saphia'd said she was heading to the Black Hills. Had she been here all this time?

Kara tightened her first around the handles of the hooks, digging her fingers into her palms. She tore her eyes away and forced herself to move on. She had to save herself before she could save anyone else, but she would free all of them. She had to. She rounded the corner to a hall full of regular doors rather than barred cells. A distinctly male groan sounded at the end of the hall.

Kara ran towards the source of the noise—more like hobbled, really. She'd seen no sign of Sanguine guards yet, but it was only a matter of time. She reached the end of the hall and froze. A familiar smell drifted under the door to her left.

She eased it open, heart going still when she saw the

mass of still muscle on a table. Dark hair in a familiar shade. Kara blinked. A stone squeezed past her throat and plunked into the abyss of her stomach. A web of frayed nerves flared across her skin.

This couldn't be happening. Kara bolted forward, barely checking the room. Logan was still as death, metal bands humming with magic wrapped around his bare torso, wrists, ankles. His eyes were closed, chest unmoving. She bent her head to his heart and waited for a beat that never came.

CHAPTER FOURTEEN

Kara shook Logan. His flesh was cold beneath her fingers, his eyes unmoving behind their lids. "Logan. Wake up! Please."

She rose a hook to his mark, which had turned the color of shadow, and ran it through the middle. His blood rose slowly. There was no flare of power, no snapping open of his eyes. A sob caught in her throat.

Kara cut her arm and parted his lips to dribble blood into his mouth. She struggled to trace the sanguinata rune from memory onto his chest. Why hadn't she practiced it, memorized it? She'd studied for a traitor instead of the man she loved. What had he done after he drew the rune?

Tears ran down her cheeks. She tried to pry off the clamps holding him down using the hook for leverage, but they held firm. They were seamless, with no keyhole. Kara lifted his limp, cold hand to her face and cradled it there.

"Please," she sobbed. She combed his face for some sign of life. She'd heard him, hadn't she? He was *here*. He had to be.

His hand vanished from her skin. He was there—the

weight and smell and sensation of him—and then he wasn't. Kara frantically touched the empty table. Even the manacles were gone.

Then the room rippled around her. The stone walls stretched and bubbled, fading into the ceiling and floor as a wooden room took shape. Victus, Salizar, and several Sanguine mercenaries appeared in a circle around her. Then the table disappeared beneath her hands.

Victus began to clap. "How was her time?"

"An hour since the door was unlocked, twenty minutes since she left the cell," Salizar said.

Victus cursed and began digging through the coin purse on his belt. "You win this time. I expected her to waste more time trying to free her sisters." Others began to exchange coin.

Kara slowly turned to Victus, blood draining from her face. She'd been played. He was the puppetmaster; she his marionette. The stranger in the dark had never been on her side. Kara started to shake, the torture and reckless flight catching up to her. She was never going to escape, never going to be free. Logan may not even be alive anymore. They were just fucking with her head.

Victus stepped toward her, and Kara raised a hook to her neck, brandishing the other in front of her. Her arm shook when she extended it.

A distant rumble filled the air. Several of the Sanguines flicked their gaze toward the corner of the room. An empty corner where no one stood. Victus held Kara's gaze.

"Logan?" she whispered.

An answering roar, though it sounded a mile away. Relief surged through her chest.

"He's breaking the illusion. Get her out of here," Salizar said.

"I want to see him," Kara said.

"I don't think you'll like what you see," Victus said.

Kara dug the hook deeper into her skin, ignoring the pain. Pain was her constant companion now. "Show me."

Victus waved his fingers at Salizar, and the illusion in the corner fell. Logan was hunched over inside a cage, kneeling on the ground. He was held up by four metal poles that riddled his body. One penetrated each shoulder and calf. The poles extended into the ceiling and the ground, preventing him from escaping them.

Kara stared in mute horror.

Both dried and fresh blood coated his skin and the inside of his cell. Logan was far paler than normal, a sunken pallor beneath his eyes, and he'd lost weight. His irises were crimson. They blazed into hers, scanning her body for damage and not liking what he saw, based on his thunderous expression.

The poles studding Logan's body began to vibrate and slide up and down. His muscles seized. He bared his teeth, the skin of his forehead tightening into furrows. Blood slid out from around the poles.

"Stop it!" Kara screamed.

"Drop your weapons," Victus said.

"No!" Logan snapped. "Don't worry about me, Kara. Save yourself." His voice crunched. He had the vocal quality of someone who'd screamed their throat raw.

Kara dropped the hooks, and Logan shut his eyes.

"Kick them over here," Victus said.

Kara did, careful to keep the sharp tips away from her bare feet.

Victus walked up to her and wrapped a hand around the back of her neck. "What do you think? Each pole has retractable barbs. It's one of my favorite toys. Most don't last long on the poles, but a Namirahn male..." Victus brushed her hair behind her shoulder. "Perhaps we'll try it on you."

Logan growled, his muscles bunching in rage. He glared at Victus like he wanted to eviscerate him. "Tell him what he wants, Kara. It will be okay."

Kara thought she'd had it bad, and all this time Logan had been enduring this abuse. Her heart clenched for him. She longed to go to him, to touch him and make sure he was real—really alive, not that lifeless illusion.

"Don't be too encouraging, Commander. You'll ruin all my fun." He gripped Kara's shoulders and spun her around, exposing the raw wounds on her back. "She's quite pretty on my hooks. Shame I'll have to find some new skin to hang her from."

A hum of rage slid from Logan, one that Kara's curse recognized and responded to in kind. Her mark flared with heat, and anger pulsed through her.

"For every scratch on her, you will suffer an eternity."

Victus laughed. "I do love a good threat."

Salizar worried his hands together. "Victus, enough. He's hard enough to manage without prancing her in front of him. He's already chewed the face off one feeding attendant."

Victus pouted his lower lip out. "I'd hoped to see if she could get his cock up. I'd like to breed him. There are so few cursed males that survive to maturity. Have you spelled him, Kara? Runed his shaft? Vakarian was never a one woman man before. Or is the pussy just that good?" Victus shoved his face against her neck and drew a deep breath. "I'm tempted to find out for myself. When you're keening and the flames lick your skin until you're a puddle of need. I have a special place in my heart for Namirahn cunts."

Kara shuddered. She'd lost track of time in her cell—

had she been here close to a month? Or was she to endure his ministrations that much longer?

Logan wrapped his hands around the poles in his shoulders and tried to pull them out of the ground, his entire body boiling with rage. When one of them inched out of the stone floor, the room grew uneasy and began to fidget.

Salizar cursed. "We need to perform the ritual soon."

"Not until the keening," Victus said.

"We have her magic eater, we don't need—"

"Enough!" Victus grabbed Kara by the arm, wrenching it as he yanked her toward the door. She held Logan's gaze as long as she could. His hand stretched out to her, eyes pained. "Kara," he groaned.

"I love you," Kara said. She should have said it to him ages ago, and now… Her throat closed up. Now might be her last chance.

Then the door shut in front of her face, blocking him from view.

Victus marched her back to her cell and tossed her in, locking it behind her. "I hope you enjoyed your little reunion. It will be your last."

()

Victus stopped visiting her after the staged escape attempt. He didn't put her on the hooks again, instead chaining her to the wall with a cuff that locked around her left ankle. Someone other than Victus brought her food and water once a day, but they always came in darkness.

Kara knew the food might be drugged or poisoned, but she had to eat to recover her strength. She struggled to keep the food down. Her back was healing slowly, and she had to sleep on her stomach on the grimy floor to protect her open wounds as best she could. Victus didn't bring her the cream that prevented infection this time, and she feared her raw skin would grow inflamed in the dirty cell.

She didn't dream of rescue anymore. Hope suffocated in her chest every time she pictured Logan and the extent of his injuries. How long could he survive like that? There were too many things left unsaid between them. But escape seemed like an impossible dream. Death might be the kindest option for them both.

Footsteps moved down the hallway, and Kara weakly rose her head. They were light footsteps, similar to those of the one who'd unlocked her cell. Had they come to gloat?

They neared the cell door and came to a stop. A small oil lantern flared to life, its warm glow throbbing against the dark. Kara blinked. An older woman with black hair streaked through with grey stood behind the bars. She wore Sanguine red, her armor a smaller, more elegant version of what the men wore. Fine lines weathered a face that was still beautiful, with hard edges and dark eyes.

The woman's penetrating gaze slid over her, leaving no inch of skin unexamined. "Have you given up already?"

Kara stayed silent, splayed out on her belly. Let her believe her defeated. If she came into her cell, she wouldn't leave. One less Sanguine for Teleria to suffer.

"Or do you lie in wait, a snake in the grass?"

Logan had once advised she attack as such, waiting for the opportune moment before striking—fast and fatal. "What do you think?" Kara's voice was hoarse from disuse, the roof of her mouth thick and cottony.

"I think Victus underestimates you, if he's only left one of your limbs chained."

Kara smiled. "Who are you?"

"A friend, and not. You may call me Magdalena. I

thought it'd be easier, but the man is not the babe he once was. And now he wears his father's face."

Kara stilled. What was the woman talking about?

"A woman came to my town when I was a child. A woman with the gift. Two brothers, she told me. One dark, one light. I chose the wrong one. The seer knew I would choose the wrong one."

Magdalena's eyes glazed over, unfocused. Lost in the past. Then she shook her head and glared at Kara, piercing her with her gaze. "Do you truly love my son?"

"Who—" Kara stilled. The woman's sharp jaw and bold brow were familiar because Kara had seen them before.

On Logan.

Ice ran through her. The mother who'd abandoned him because of his mark, who'd wanted to kill him rather than raise a Namirahn son. A Sanguine captain who'd been with the clan for all of Victus's atrocities.

"I don't think you know what love is."

Logan's mother gripped the barred door with iron fingers. "Everything I did, I did for love. One son would be the death of another. One would bring light, one dark. I knew what Namirah's mark meant. I knew he had to die."

Unease flickered through Kara's stomach as it flopped over, sadness for Logan squeezing her heart. This woman had put the ravings of a seer above her own son.

"Who is the second son?" Logan had never spoken of a brother, but he hadn't seen his mother since he was a baby, when his father escaped with him.

"Victus." The name slid out with a sigh. A secret whispered into the dark.

Kara's mind rebelled. Harder than when Calim had shown her the portrait of Namirah, harder than when she'd seen Da's head clenched in Cervus's fist. They couldn't share blood. The man who'd trained her and loved her and the man who'd tortured them both to the breaking point?

Her mind twisted away from the answer at the same time it sought a solution. Victus, enamored of the power of Namirah's Chosen. The power his brother possessed. He'd gathered so many of the chosen. A ripple of terror wove through Kara's belly. He'd kept everyone alive—even given Kara a break from his ministrations. What was he planning to do?

"How?" Logan's father had broken from the Sanguines, escaped with his son, and formed the Stygian clan.

"The only blood they share is mine. Victus's father is the former Sanguine commander. But the boy is a shadow of his father, where Logan is an eclipse. I was wrong. I was so wrong. Why did I believe her?" Magdalena clenched the bars and shook her head.

Kara bit her lip. She would bargain with this woman if it might mean their freedom. "And are your prepared to try and remedy your mistakes?"

"Victus grows reckless, his thirst for power insatiable. Sometimes a rabid dog needs to be put down."

"I will do all I can to kill him, but you have to save Logan—have you seen what Victus has done to him? He won't survive much longer like that. Please. He is your son."

The woman—Kara hesitated to think of her as Logan's mother—tilted her head to the side. "You beg for his escape before your own. Curious." All emotion had disappeared from her voice, as if she'd shoved a lid on them, snuffing them out. "And if I were to offer you a choice? Yourself or my son?"

"Logan."

"You don't even take the time to think about it?" Magdalena huffed through her nostrils. "Fool. One has to be for themselves first in this world, or you'll never be able to help anyone else."

"Is that logic what got you where you are today? We both know Victus will never let me go. And your son—your first son—is a good man. You can make up for the past."

The woman's lips pursed. "Logan will refuse to leave without you. Just like his father."

Kara took a deep breath and closed her eyes. She knew it was true. He'd happily fight and die to free her, but he'd suffered so much already. "Then let him believe the worst."

"Now you are beginning to understand."

Kara couldn't stop the broken laugh that bubbled up in her throat. "You're a true credit to the title mercenary."

Magdalena picked up her lantern and turned to leave, and Kara called out, "Wait. My brother. Wesley McKenna. Is he here?"

Magdalena turned toward Kara. "Are you sure you want to know the answer?"

Kara nodded with a quick jerk of her head. She'd help him out of this if he needed—wanted—her help, but she had to know if it was for naught.

"That one walks a dark path. He tends your beloved."

Bile bubbled up in the back of Kara's throat, and she forced it down. She wouldn't hesitate to kill Wesley this time if he forced her hand.

CHAPTER FIFTEEN

They came for her two days after Magdalena's visit. Victus led Salizar and two helmeted Sanguines down the dark tunnel to her cell.

"Kara, Kara. How are you finding the dark? Rejoice! You won't have to linger in it any longer after today," Victus said.

"I'll rejoice when I've got the taste of your lifesblood in my throat."

The four of them laughed. "So vicious, so feral. However did you blend in at court? Oh right. You didn't." Victus unlocked the cell and stepped aside, motioning for the others to enter.

Kara scrambled away from them, but the two guards backed her into a corner and secured her by the arms. Salizar bent to unlock her cuffed ankle, and Kara jerked her knee up, catching him in the face.

Salizar cursed and fell away. "Godsdamnedit, hold her fucking legs, you imbeciles."

The guards grunted and locked their legs around Kara's, holding her still.

Salizar rose and brushed off his robes. Kara smiled when she saw the swollen patch of skin around his eye.

He backhanded her across the face, and the sharp ring he wore tore her skin in a ragged streak of fire. He lifted the ring to his mouth and sucked her blood off it.

Victus hissed. "Don't fucking touch her again, or I'll have your hands. We've come too far to risk this." Victus shoved Salizar away and knelt to unlock her ankle cuff. He ran a hand down the inside of her leg as he bent, and Kara shuddered. She hated the growing number of physical similarities she recognized between him and Logan.

He rose to his feet and gripped her jaw, running his thumb across her cheek. "You see him in me, don't you? His power should have been mine. He could have been so much more."

Kara tried to twist her head to bite him, and his grip tightened, holding her fast.

"I wanted to delay this until your keening, but you have tenacious friends."

Kara stopped struggling as they carried her out of the cell. Tenacious friends? Were the Stygians close to finding them? She knew they'd look—for Logan if not for her—but she'd had little hope of being found in time, since their attempts to locate Victus's prison were fruitless in the past. If she could delay, it might give them time to arrive.

The guards dragged Kara up the ladder and down the upper cellblock. Kara's stomach dropped when they passed Saphia's cell. She hung in the same place, but now she bore an ugly wound on her cheek where someone had sliced the magic eater out of her. It would scar, badly.

They walked down the hallway that'd held Logan until they arrived at a large central chamber with several paths branching off it. The ceiling was curved stone, the hallways rough tunnels that looked like they'd been formed by a rockworm's burrowing.

The cavernous room had a deep, sunken pit in the middle lined with barrels arranged in a spiral. A stone slab with metal cuffs bolted to it sat in the middle. Kara swallowed thickly when she saw the intricate rune carved into bottom of the pit. It was the largest she'd ever seen, some forty feet across, forming interlocking paths between the barrels and the stone slab.

The Sanguine guards dangled Kara over the pit and dropped her. She fell several feet, stumbling to her bruised knees against the rough stone. She scrabbled up and ran to the other side, determined to climb a barrel and try to jump to the pit's edge.

She glanced up and jerked to a stop. Sanguines appeared from every hallway branching out from the chamber, slowly closing in. There were hundreds of them —men and women, young and old. A sea of red metal encircled her. Victus and Salizar stood at the edge of the pit and looked down. Kara's knees shook.

"You understand your situation now, I see," Victus said. He snapped his fingers, and a group of Sanguine mercenaries parted. Four large men carried Logan to the edge of the pit. He appeared unconscious, head sunken down, his body riddled with bruises, streaks of blood, and the insidious dark holes from the poles Victus had rigged him on. Victus's guards carried him to a metal chair and cuffed him into it, securing his arms and ankles.

"I thought he might like to watch," Victus said with a smile. Then he drew his sword and rested it on the back of Logan's neck.

Kara's heart constricted. She forced her battered body into a run. She'd kill as many as she could before they brought her down—

Victus held out a hand. "Stop. If you want him to live, however briefly, you will turn around and secure yourself to the stone."

Kara halted. More of Victus's games. She scoured the eyes of the Sanguine onlookers, looking for a friendly face. Where was Magdalena, Wesley? Anyone who might help her. Stony expressions met hers.

"I don't need him alive for my purposes," Victus said. He applied pressure with his sword, and a dark red line welled on Logan's neck.

"Okay!" Kara stumbled back toward the stone. She climbed onto it, closing the cuffs around her ankles first. They snapped shut with force, like they were eager to close, and the hum of magic sizzled around her lower body. Kara laid back. Her eyes shot open in pain as her flayed back met the rough stone. As soon as she positioned her wrists within their cuffs, they snapped closed on their own.

Kara's heart beat wildly. Magic arced across her skin, creeping up her throat and down the roots of her hair. It had the same familiar sting as the magic they'd used to mute her voice in Travincal.

Salizar lowered himself into the pit with a rope. He walked to the first barrel in rune's spiral and tapped it, then moved to the next and repeated the process. Kara heard the steady drip of liquid against the floor of the pit, but she couldn't see what came out, still circled by an inner ring of barrels. Maybe they'd drown her in well-aged whiskey.

Salizar went barrel by barrel, and the slow drip became a steady patter. Dark red fluid ran down the rune lines carved deep into the stone, inching towards Kara.

At first Kara thought it was wine, and then the old, coppery scent hit her nose.

Blood. Barrels and barrels of blood.

Kara cast her eyes around the pit, searching for any runes she might recognize within the larger sprawl. What spell required this much blood?

Salizar tapped the final barrel and turned to her, a twisted smile on his face. "I must thank you again, my dear, for being so accommodating as to take the magic eater of your own volition. Really sped up our timeline. You squandered your power, your heritage, but now it will serve a greater purpose." Salizar climbed out of the pit and pulled up his rope.

Blood reached the edge of Kara's stone. She looked at Logan, willing him to wake up. If these were going to be her final moments, she wanted to say goodbye.

The acrid scent of magic eaters clogged the air as blood flooded the pit. Horror bloomed in her gut. That smell…the marked women Victus had been capturing for years. It was all connected. He'd been harvesting the magic in their bodies to prepare for this, this ritual. What the fuck required this much power? And they had the magic eater Kara had nursed, the one empowered by Namirah's blood.

The blood reached Kara, creeping across the stone to pool along her skin. It drenched her hair and slid beneath her until she was soaked with it.

The Sanguines stared on in silence. A raw, crackling energy suffused the room. Kara's head spun.

"It's time," Salizar said.

Logan's head began to nod as two Sanguine guards gripped his hands and pried them open, palms up toward the ceiling. Then Salizar drug a dagger through Logan's wrists, and Kara screamed. Not Logan. Not like this.

Logan's head jerked up, eyes flaring red as he took in the scene. He was still disoriented—hadn't even looked down at his wrists yet. Lifeblood dripped down the side of the pit, joining the rest of Namirah's Chosen.

"Logan! Save yourself, please—" She didn't know how it was possible. At this point, what could anyone do, even Magdalena?

Logan's eyes found hers, and the chair shook as he pulled at his bonds. His blood spilled faster. He glanced down, finally realizing what was happening. When his eyes met hers again, they were heavy with finality.

"I love you, Kara. Thank you for everything. May you meet me in your dreams."

Kara unleashed a keening wail full of pain and longing. Full of everything she hadn't had a chance to say. Tears bled down her cheeks, and she shook in her bonds.

Logan's marked wrist began to heal, slowly stitching closed, and Salizar sliced through it again. Logan's skin paled as blood poured out of him. His eyes never left hers, as if he wanted to soak up as much of her as he could in the time they had left. Again and again Salizar sliced through his healing mark, until it no longer flared with power.

"Stay with me, Logan." She turned to Victus and begged. "Stop. Don't do this. I'll do whatever you want, just let him go."

Victus tsked and shook his head. "Too little too late, darling. I'm afraid you've served your purpose." Victus jumped into the pit and strode towards Kara, wading through the crimson lake.

The blood surged as Logan's mixed with it, the magic in the air growing thicker. All the hair on Kara's body rose.

Victus leaned over her and drew his dagger. He slid it through Kara's mark with a smile on his face. She stared, numb, as vital blood left her body, joining that of her sisters and her lover. Of all those Victus had hurt. Her mark flared a demonic red color. Then the blood level in the pit rose rapidly, far faster than it should have given the flow and capacity of the barrels. Victus climbed back out of the pit and looked on eagerly, a manic energy in his eyes. Salizar had abandoned Logan to bleed and was kneeling at the edge of the pit as if in prayer.

Logan nodded off and slumped forward, eyes losing focus. Kara fought against the manacles holding her down, screaming, her mind clawing for anything she could do to prevent this—to save him.

Magic buzzed across her back as the blood coated her, and the pain there eased. The same thing happened at her battered wrists and ankles—every scrape and bruise she'd acquired during her time in the dungeons began to heal, including where Victus had cut into her mark.

The blood flooded her ears, then the corners of her eyes, still rising steadily. She lifted her head as far as she was able. It almost covered her calves now.

She refused to die choking on the blood of her tortured brethren, Logan slowly bleeding out, Victus and Salizar still alive. They needed to die. *Deserved to die.* She yanked at her wrists until her skin burned. *Fuck! Think, Kara.* Magic energy choked the room, and it hit her. Power. She could use her power. This room couldn't be rune blocked, she was strapped down in the middle of a giant one.

Kara stretched her blood-soaked fingers in a painful, awkward bend, carefully tracing the rune for *unlock* on her right cuff. All four cuffs restraining her sprung open. She stood, and the blood that slid off her gathered and rose into a shape. It was a pillar of dark liquid at first, shuddering in the air, and then its edges began to twist and curve.

Kara stumbled backwards and tripped, falling into the crimson lake. It tugged at her, pulling her down. She ripped away from its cloying grasp.

She tried to run, to reach the edge of the pit and

Logan. A hundred bloody hands reached out for her, pulling her down with each step.

Kara looked back to the pillar in the center of the altar. It had flattened into a large oval rippling at the edges like a flag in the wind. The space it occupied felt *wrong*, unnatural.

The oval shuddered and flattened, and then Kara stared at a reflection of herself tinted red.

Skin began to melt off her mirror self, starting at her mark, revealing ethereal flesh that glowed red underneath. Faster and faster it vanished, up to the roots of her hair and the tips of her toes. Hair fell away like ash, and ebony horns ruptured from her forehead, growing until they swept back behind her ears. Her brow jutted forward into a sharp point.

Eyes bled and grew until they glowed like rubies. Kara rose a quivering hand to her head and touched normal hair and skin. Her reflection mirrored her movements with the black talons that had sprouted from their fingertips.

Then a taller creature stepped into the mirror behind her reflection. It was male, riddled with muscle and cock swinging between its legs. His horns stood high, curving back over his prominent brow. His claws curled over her mirror demon's shoulder, and a sharp-edged tail curled around her waist.

Kara gasped when she felt the tiny pinpricks of lethal claws on her skin. *Logan.* It had to be. Some part of him was still alive in there, beyond that rippling veil of blood.

'*Join us*' echoed through her mind in a slithered whisper. It was Logan's voice, but ancient, archaic—like the crackle of burning logs in a great fire. The male's tail trailed between the female's thighs, and Kara felt its phantom flicker across her own skin.

She took a step toward her reflection, and the demon

couple's lips curved in serrated smiles. They wanted her to join them. Better to live in their realm than die in this one.

A wave rippled over the mirror, and a blood-soaked hand clenching a ruby crystal thrust out of it. The fingers opened one by one, dropping the crystal into the pool of blood. The demons' gaze jerked toward it.

Someone called Kara, the sound a distant buzz beyond the cacophony of magic.

Kara took a step forward, lured by some force she didn't understand, and clasped the grasping hand in hers. She half expected to be pulled forward, but the mirror rippled in earnest, the demons fading. The hand tightened around hers, blood slick and sticky, jagged nails digging into her skin.

"*Free me,*" a familiar voice whispered. She'd heard it before. Blown on a forest wind through the Blackshear as she rushed towards Widow's Fall. Leading her to an altar drenched with magic in the royal forest.

Kara tried to let go, to step back, but the grip was iron. Her feet slid toward the mirror.

"*You must resist.*"

Kara wasn't sure if she should trust the voice or not, but she struggled with the hand like she had the largest fish in the lake fighting on the line. She braced her legs and pulled. An elbow appeared from the swirling reflection. Kara heaved.

The portal ripped open, and the resistance disappeared. Kara's feet slid out from under her. Blood flooded her mouth and nostrils as her head went under. Panic spiked through her. She struggled to her feet, spitting viciously to clear her tongue of the coppery, sparking flavor.

A woman stood before her, coated in blood. *Made of blood?* There was no way to tell. Everything was wet and red and dripping. Then she opened her eyes, and the fire of Namirah's Chosen burned out.

The woman bent over and coughed. A stream of dark blood poured from her lips. She lifted and swiped her hands over her face, revealing patches of pale skin beneath the crimson swathes.

The face she revealed was familiar, uncannily so. But it couldn't be…

Namirah. It was the face from the portrait. Unchanged, as if she'd sat for it yesterday.

Impossible.

"You—you died."

"Indeed. Second birth is highly overrated."

Kara's mind rebelled. "How?"

Namirah waved one blood-soaked hand in a casual shrug. "I intend to find out."

Kara stared in mute horror.

Namirah braced her hands on her hips and looked around the chamber.

"Well, it's not exactly the royal welcome, but I've had enough of royals, don't you think?" Her gaze fell to Kara. "Granddaughter. You wear my likeness well."

Kara's breath caught on a sob. What had she done? Her gaze skirted tot he swirling pattern of barrels studding the pit. It was all beginning to make horrible sense. Victus's focus on finding her, his mutterings about the bloodline. He and Salizar had brought Namirah back somehow— resurrected her using the power they harvested from hundreds of cursed women. From Kara.

She blinked, remembering where they were, who surrounded them. Her head snapped to Logan. He was slumped forward in his chair, unnaturally still and pale. Blood no longer leaked from the dark slices through his wrists. Ice slithered through Kara's veins.

No.

Kara ran towards the wall of the pit as fast as the deep liquid would allow. The pool of blood no longer resisted her steps.

Victus was wading through the pit towards Namirah, his gaze reverent. He didn't spare Kara a glance.

She leapt for the lip of the pit and fell woefully short. She tried again, and a hand caught her arm and dragged her up. Green eyes gazed down at her from behind a Sanguine helm.

Kara's heart tripped as she was lifted to her feet. Wesley was here, helping her. Perhaps she *had* gone through the portal, and this was a world where everything that ought not be was. Perhaps she was still hanging from the hooks in her cell, lost to an elaborate fever dream.

Kara squeezed Wesley's hand and nodded at him, then ran for Logan. None of the Sanguines tried to stop her; many of them were missing. Shouts and the peal of metal striking metal rung out from one of the corridors.

Wesley strode after her. "Your friends are here, Kara. You must go to them while Victus is distracted. Logan's gone."

Victus had reached Namirah and knelt, thigh-deep in the pit of blood. Namirah was staring at her hands as if she didn't recognize them, flipping them over and flexing her fingers.

"My queen," Victus said, head bowed. "I am your loyal servant. The one who engineered your resurrection, gathered the power necessary to pull you from the shadow realm."

Kara reached Logan and clutched his face, lifting his head. It swung listlessly, his neck no longer supporting him. She pressed her hand to his chest, waiting for a heartbeat, a breath, *anything* but the jagged pain scratching at her soul.

His eyes were empty, staring at nothing. The life gone out of them.

Kara's scream rent the air.

It wasn't possible. He was so strong, so full of life. They couldn't end like this.

She traced the sanguinata onto his chest with fumbling fingers, but her memory of the rune's shape was muddled.

Wesley gripped her shoulder and tried to pull her back. "Kara, we have to go. He's gone."

She ripped away from him. "No! I have to try. He can't —he can't be gone." Her voice broke.

She yanked Wesley's dagger from his waist and sliced through her mark, then held it to Logan's mouth. Blood pooled on his tongue, but no swallow ever came. Tears blurred her vision. She tilted his head back and cradled it to her chest. "Please, Logan. You can't leave me. Not like this—not ever. I love you. I should have told you I loved you."

She was splitting open, an internal rupture tearing wider every second he didn't blink. Inhale. Flash her a pained grin, more worried about her than being at death's door. This was worse than flaying her back open on Victus's hooks, worse than any of it. Her soul was shattering.

She traced the sanguinata again, then the runes for healing over his empty wrists. Again and again she drew, until the shapes were indistinct and tears blurred her vision. Swipes of red littered his body.

Wesley gripped her by the waist and tried to lift her away, but she fought him off with wild swings of the dagger.

"Wesley, shut her up. We no longer need her," Victus said.

Namirah's flaming gaze jerked to Victus. Shadows

pulsed around her, and the blood at her feet swirled in ominous eddies. "You dare to kill my brethren? The blood of my blood? My only living descendant?"

Victus sputtered. "She's loyal to our enemy, my queen. I've tried to convert her, but she will never be true to our cause."

"She brought me here by her own hand, as you saw. That was her choice to make."

"Look inside my mind. You will see what I say is true. She is nothing. She wastes your gift. *I* am worthy of your power. Your curse. You will see."

Namirah gripped the top of Victus's skull in her palm and closed her eyes. Her lips curled into a severe frown, eyes jerking behind her lids. She gasped, eyes snapping open. "Worthy? You tortured my chosen, harvested power not freely given and tainted with their pain. You mutilated my granddaughter for your own pleasure, murdered her lover—your own brother. You are no better than Urian. You were a useful worm, but your use is at its end."

Kara's mind balked at her words. Logan *wasn't* dead. She refused a reality without him in it.

Victus tried to shake his head and rise. Namirah tightened her grip. The flesh of her hand melted away like Kara's mirror image's had, revealing a glowing red core. Her fingers grew and lengthened, and black claws climbed from her nailbeds.

Victus howled in pain as her talons grew into his skull. Then Namirah squeezed her hand into a fist, and Victus's skull collapsed with a sickening crunch. Blood and skull fragments sprayed out. His neck ended in a mass of red pulp.

Namirah released him and shook the gore off her hand as it shrunk back to normal size and the claws receded, skin rapidly coating it again. Victus's body fell backwards into the pool of blood.

Kara was only sorry it hadn't been her to kill him, to feel his bones break beneath her fingers.

She met Namirah's gaze and played her final card.

"Grandmother, if you bear me any love—if you bore your daughter any love before she died at Urian's hands—grant me this boon. Save him. My parents died for your legacy before they even took root in my memory."

Namirah's head tilted to the side, her gaze reptilian. "You no longer deny your heritage?"

Kara's laugh was broken. "You wear my face. How can I? Our blood brought you back; we freed you from death. Save him. Please. He's my soul."

"Part of it, perhaps. But never your whole soul, darling. Never give them your whole soul. Then what will be left of you when they leave? That demon in the mirror. And no qualms about wearing human skin."

Is that what had happened to her, after Urian betrayed her?

Namirah took a step, and the blood gathered beneath her in a wave that lifted her out of the pit and carried her to Kara's side. She spread her palm over Logan's brow, and Kara's fingers tightened on her dagger.

Namirah gripped Logan's jaw in her fist and looked at Kara. "This one? You're sure?"

"Yes."

"The shadow of death hangs over him; he sits astride the realms. The man is barely there, but the demon lingers. He is strong. Worthy of you, perhaps."

The fighting in the hallway sounded closer now. A few Sanguines emerged from it, blood smearing their armor. They glanced at Victus's headless corpse floating at the bottom of the pit and kept running.

"Your blade, please."

Kara passed her the dagger.

"If I do this for you, blood of my blood, then I will ask a boon in return. I will call upon you for a favor in the future."

Kara nodded. "Anything." She knew she wouldn't like the price she'd be asked to pay, but Namirah was right. Logan already had her whole soul, and losing him would break her.

"Kara—" Wesley said.

Kara cut her eyes to him. "Shut up, Wesley."

"Swear it in blood," Namirah said.

Kara clasped Namirah's bloody hand in hers. "I swear it. I owe you a boon."

Namirah sliced through her left arm, which bore the same mark as all of her chosen. She held her wrist to Logan's mouth and looked down at his bared chest. "You must work on your runes. I will train you." She made several bloody swipes through one of Kara's runes, creating one that Kara didn't recognize. More swipes, and Logan's bindings snapped open.

Kara stared at Logan, willing him back to life. Imagining a link between them that traded her life force for his.

A shadow flickered over Logan's skin and settled into it. For a small eternity, nothing happened. He was still, breathless. His chest didn't rise and fall, his eyes didn't burn through her with their fire. A sob crawled its way up Kara's throat. She dug her nails into her palms until her skin split.

Then Logan's eyes snapped wide, and he drew in a deep, gasping breath. Like he'd been yanked back to life.

Kara threw herself at him, wrapping around him in a hug that squeezed his ribs together.

He groaned at the contact and returned the embrace, fingers curling weakly around her waist.

"I thought I lost you," she whispered into his neck. The tears she'd been holding back began to fall in great, wracking sobs, and her body shook against his.

He pressed his lips against her brow so hard she could feel his teeth behind them. "I'm right here, love. I'm not going anywhere."

Kara took a ragged breath. "How do you feel?"

"Like I had a very nice nap. Peaceful. Dark. There was a very good-looking demon fellow—"

She resisted the urge to punch him in the arm. "I love you, Logan Vakarian."

"You don't know how long I've been waiting to hear you say that. To hold you in my arms as it falls from your lips."

Kara pulled back and pressed her forehead against his. Something sharp poked her arm, and she frowned and pulled away.

Large black spikes were growing from Logan's shoulders, filling the gaping holes Victus's torture had left and curving along his back like thorns on a flower.

Kara's gaze snapped to Namirah. She should have known better than to trust her. "What's happening to him?"

"A side effect of my demon-rich blood. The muscles and tendons in those areas were torn, shredded over and over and thick with scar tissue. The blood improvised, adapted."

"I can feel them growing out the back of my calves, too. I'll have to have all my clothes tailored."

Feet soldiered up the hallway.

"Cavalry's here!" Jon's voice rung out as he burst into the room, his face streaked with blood.

A mob of people rushed in behind him, weapons drawn and at the ready. Thomas's glaive was dark with blood, and his glasses hung crooked on his face. Serena carried two swords, one burning with starlight and the other smoking obsidian. George carried a spiked club still matted with flesh and hair. Rahj held no weapon, but blood coated his arms and he looked drained, his face tight with exhaustion. More familiar faces filtered in behind them, including Jasper and Bear. So the lordling had remained loyal after all.

"You're late, second."

"See, I told you he'd be alive. Like a roach, that one—survives anything."

Several faces swung between Kara and Namirah, then back again, their lips parting.

"Mother Night," Jon said.

"Spitting image," George whispered.

"Goddess save us." Aaron crossed his hands in the ward sign against evil.

"Any casualties?" Logan asked.

Jon's face fell, and Kara winced. How quickly Logan resumed the burden of leadership.

Faedra and Feron drug a makeshift litter into the room. Athar rested on it, a quickly spreading stain across his abdomen.

Kara swallowed the lump in her throat and glanced at Serena. "We can't heal him?"

Serena shook her head. "The wound is bad—infection's already in his blood. I don't have the power."

Kara climbed out of Logan's lap and moved to Athar. "I can try—"

Athar took a deep, rattling breath. "Keep your blood, missy. You need it more than me. I know a lethal gut wound when I see one—pulled my own sword out of enough of 'em." His breath rattled. "I got the one that did it, that's what matters. It's time for me to go home. See my Martha again."

Jon turned away and lowered his head, eyes clouded with tears.

Namirah took everything in with a curious gaze.

Sanguine armor flashed in the dark as a woman rushed to Athar's side.

All the weapons swung to point at her, keeping her out of reach of Athar. Logan pulled Kara back against him.

The Sanguine reached for her helm with shaking arms and drew it off, and a mane of black streaked with grey fell out.

"Lena?" Athar gasped.

Logan's body went still against Kara. "Mother," he whispered, so low no one else could possibly hear.

Kara glanced at him. He'd been a babe when they'd separated. There was no way he'd remember what she looked like…unless he had sought her out once he was older. Kara's heart clenched. Had she rejected him then, too?

Athar's great chest shook in a strained, wet laugh. "I told you I'd be seeing you again, girly."

"I hadn't imagined it like this, old man. I believe you had me at the end of a blade at the time."

He waved a hand at the drawn weapons. "Enough. She's not gonna kill me any faster, and if she did it'd be a mercy."

The pack of bristling edges slowly lowered, but everyone kept their weapons drawn and at the ready.

Magdalena crawled to Athar's side and took his large, hairy hand between hers. "I'm glad you went with him. For supporting him when I didn't. Thank you for keeping my son safe. I know he benefited from your guidance. You did what I was too much of a coward to do."

"It's not too late to fix things, Lena."

She stroked a hand over Athar's face and nodded. "I'll try."

Logan stood on shaky legs and moved to Athar. He knelt at his side and stroked a hand through his hair, cradling Athar's head in his palm. He carefully avoided his mother's gaze. Kara stood beside Logan and squeezed his shoulder.

"Thank you for your love, your loyalty, and your service. Tell dad I said hello."

Athar nodded. "He'd be proud, Logan. You've made both of us so proud." Athar's eyes drifted shut.

Kara bit her lip as tears leaked down her cheeks.

"Give your mother a chance. It'd do you both good. And tell Rohan he won this one."

Athar did not go out of this world quietly, but with a great, shuddering breath that fluttered across his beard.

Magdalena broke down into sobs.

Logan pulled Athar's black Stygian cloak around him, laid his sword on his chest, and crossed his arms over the pommel. One by one, the Stygians knelt and paid their respects to their quartermaster.

CHAPTER SIXTEEN

Their group camped in the Black Hills, not far from the hidden prison. They hadn't been able to travel far. They needed to tend to the wounded, including the forty-odd women freed from Victus's prison. They were in a poor state, heavily wounded in body or spirit both. Some of them still bore magic eaters they'd need help to remove. Jon and Faedra interviewed the women, asking after their families and where they lived so they might help them return home at long last. A few expressed interest in joining the Stygians if it meant an opportunity to draw more Sanguine blood. Others pledged their service to Namirah, drawn to the resurrected enchantress like moths to a flame.

The women who'd chosen to side with Victus rather than endure torture were pardoned, but they were not welcome to stay. They would make their way to other climes or perhaps join the Sanguines again, once their new leader emerged. A large faction of the Sanguine Riders were killed during the prison break, but the clan would still be a force to be reckoned with.

Who would take over with Victus gone was still up in the air. Many of the high-ranking officers had been there for Namirah's resurrection. Kara wondered if Magdalena would make a play for power.

They did not find Salizar among the fallen bodies, and Kara feared he'd escaped in the chaos. Had he kept any of her magic eater for himself, or dedicated it all to the summoning? The last time she'd seen him, before all the chaos, he'd knelt at the edge of the ritual pit, reverence in his gaze. He was not done with Namirah.

Kara huddled in her and Logan's tent alone, rubbing her hands together for warmth as her teeth chattered. She couldn't stop shivering. Rahj and Serena sat by the fire outside, discussing how to collapse the prison with magic so it couldn't be used again. The reason the hideout had been so difficult to locate had become clear when they'd emerged—the majority of the structure was buried underground, the entrance formed of sculpted earth that looked no different from the thousands of other hills that gave the Black Hills their name. There were also runes around the perimeter meant to obfuscate and confuse anyone seeking the place out.

Kara was tempted to peek outside the tent and look for Logan. Any time he was out of her sight, her chest grew tight and she felt short of breath. Like saving him had been a dream, or temporary, or Namirah would take it all back the moment she got the chance. Kara hadn't recognized the improvised rune Namirah used on Logan, but she knew better than to trust the sorceress, blood relation or not.

The tent flap opened, and Logan ducked inside.

Kara released the breath she'd been holding.

"I'd thought to come warm up by your side, but you

look like an icicle." He shook out the roll of furs he carried and laid them down for them to curl up between.

"How do you feel?" Kara asked.

"Like I got in a fight with a bullmoose and lost."

Logan wrapped around her, pulling her against him, and drew the fur up to her cheek.

Kara burrowed her face in his chest, hands diving beneath his shirt so she could feel his skin. She wanted to crawl inside him.

"What's wrong? You were looking rather forlorn."

"I'm scared. I thought I was going to lose you—I *did* lose you. You were gone, Logan. I don't know how she brought you back from the brink, and I'm afraid there's going to be a consequence I haven't thought of yet. I'm afraid it's not going to last."

"We'll cross that road when we come to it. I can feel her magic inside me still. It's…indescribable. Heady like summer wine and the elation of catching yourself just before you fall."

"I'm not certain we can count her as an ally."

"No, I daresay we can't. She's got an agenda and enough power to shake the kingdom. We'd be fools to trust her."

Kara traced her hands down the sharp spikes curling behind Logan's shoulders.

"Do you like them?"

"They'll be good weapons, and I'm glad you're healed. Though I imagine you'll be punching holes in your bed sheets to begin with. How do you feel about them?"

"I'm just happy to be here. With you."

Kara closed her eyes. She had so many questions, all of them difficult to broach. Her mind had already begun the work of trying to distance herself from the events in the dungeon, though they returned nightly to visit her in her dreams.

"Did you know about Victus?" She whispered into the dark.

"That he was my brother, you mean?"

Kara nodded.

"I had suspicions, but never confirmation. Not until his sessions with me. The fool was jealous of the curse, its power. I'm so sorry, Kara. The things he did to you—" Logan's fingers traced the hard ridges along her back where Kara's flesh had rapidly knit closed. His jaw tightened, eyes flashing amber. "My only regret is that I wasn't the one to kill him."

"Don't apologize. You suffered even more than I."

"I've never felt so helpless. He was hurting you right in front of me, and there was nothing I could do to stop it. I thought I was going to lose you. My demon has never ridden me so close as in those moments."

"What about Magdalena? Are you going to give her a chance?"

"It was Athar's dying wish. I will try, for his sake."

Kara still wasn't sure what to think of Lena. After they'd escaped the prison and set up camp, Jon had briefed them on everything they'd missed during their capture. They'd only been able to find the fortress because Wesley had sent a letter to Raven's Rest detailing nearby landmarks, and Rohan relayed that information. Wesley's fate was still uncertain, considering his past betrayal, but he was allowed at the camp for now. Kara wasn't ready to talk to him yet, and Logan had threatened to flay him if he came near her without her permission.

Lena had helped in her own way, adjusting guard schedules and unlocking doors to aid the Stygian's entrance. Reports from Lerathil were grim. Ariana had seized power with the help of the Sanguines and Prince Rand, and Calim's whereabouts were unknown.

Kara closed her eyes and tried to quiet her mind, relishing the warm silence, the feel of Logan's skin against hers and the reassuring beat of his heart thrumming through her.

"We need a holiday."

"I've an estate to the east of Briarcliff. It's quite picturesque, so I'm assured."

Kara snorted. "You've never even visited it? The place is likely looted and in shambles."

Logan shook his head. "I've staffed people to manage the estate's finances and assist the tenants. I don't have time for much else."

Kara rolled her eyes. "Well, Lord Melbourne. If you wish to wile away the summer in the country, I shan't argue."

"Reaping will be soon." His breath hitched, and he tightened his hold on her and breathed into her hair. "With Athar gone, I'll need to fill a spot on the recruitment panel."

"Do you have anyone in mind?"

"As a matter of fact," he began, kissing down chest and belly and spreading her legs. "I do."

"Who?"

Logan chuckled and ran his nose along her inner thigh. "Isn't it obvious?"

"Not much is obvious when you're touching me like that."

"It's someone new to the clan, actually."

"Oh?"

"Mhmm. Soon to be reinducted."

Kara's heart swelled. "Really?"

"Yes, my love. If you want to come back, of course. I

hear there's this Lord Melbourne fellow who'd like to retire you to the country and spend the days rutting and drinking wine instead."

"A tempting proposition."

"I'll just have to make staying worth your while."

Kara spread her legs wider and arched her back as he laved her core with his long tongue. "You're off to a fine start."

()

CALIM ARRIVED at their camp the next day, to everyone's relief. He led a contingent of royal army members that remained loyal following Ariana's insurrection. Aidan was among them.

"You're late!" Jon yelled.

Calim ignored him, scanning the campground for something. His eyes were frenzied, and his horse pranced under his nervous hands. "Where is she? Someone told me she was here."

"Who?" Jon asked.

"Saphia!"

Kara paused. "Saphia Kingslayer?"

A terse nod.

"She's recovering, Calim. Whatever grudge you may bear can wait."

He glared at her, worry obvious in the tightness of his eyes and heavy shadows beneath them. Kara began to wonder just how Saphia had come by the moniker *Kingslayer*.

"I see. She's in the healer's tent. Follow me."

Calim swung off his horse tracked her to the makeshift infirmary. He zeroed in on Saphia as soon as they entered, rushing to her side and kneeling. Saphia was bruised and waif thin, with a brutal, puckered scar beneath her left cheek, but Serena had assured them she'd make a full physical recovery. Healing the mind was another matter, and many of Victus's victims would bear those scars for the rest of their lives.

Calim pushed Saphia's ashen, sweat-damp hair behind her ear and kissed her on her brow. Her hands were small and pale in his large palms.

Saphia's brilliant blue eyes fluttered open. "You came," she croaked.

"I told you I would."

"You always were absentminded," Saphia said, "But I didn't expect you to lose the entire kingdom."

Calim's laugh was slightly deranged. He was infatuated, and he'd believed the worst. Kara slid out of the tent, allowing them the little privacy the infirmary allowed.

"That one has the look of Genevieve's get," a honeyed voice said. "The former King Calim, I presume?"

Kara bristled and swung to Namirah. "You're not to touch him."

"I vowed to end Urian's line, and I intend to finish the job. No touching need be involved."

"Am I not of Urian's line, then?"

"You're of *my* line. The others are not so lucky."

"Are you determined to make enemies of us so quickly? Calim is a good man."

Namirah glanced toward the tent with a distant, glazed look that often came over her. As if part of her were still beyond that crimson veil. "Perhaps. I shall take his measure."

Logan and Aidan approached the twin women, as disparate as the sun and moon. The golden god and the beast of night.

Aidan nodded at Kara. "Celine. Err—Kara, is it? I'm glad to see you're well."

Kara flushed. She hadn't considered the fallout of her true identity being revealed to others from court.

Aidan gave her a small grin. "We're due for another spar. One where you don't hold back, this time." His gaze fell to Namirah, and his eyes popped open. His throat bobbed with a rough swallow. "I should go help Calim." Aidan hurried off towards the wrong tent.

Logan wrapped himself around Kara from behind and lowered his mouth to her ear. "I believe you've left the viscount speechless."

Kara snorted. "I ought to dye my hair. How long before someone tries to kill me because we wear the same face?"

Logan frowned and traced a finger down her cheek. "Perhaps a large facial tattoo?"

AFTER ALLOWING Victus's victims time to recover, the party began making preparations for the journey back to Raven's Rest. Serena and Rahj ensured Athar's body would last the return journey, so he could be could be laid to rest on friendly soil.

"You're welcome to come with us," Logan told Calim. The deposed king had been doting on Saphia like a mother hen, sleeping by her side in the infirmary on a lumpy cot and ferrying cool water and hot tea to her at the slightest shift in her condition.

Calim's eyes skittered over Namirah, perched on her horse in the distance. "Thank you, but I'm not sure that's a good idea."

"Then stay safe, friend. We'll be in touch."

"When the time comes, I'll need your help to recover the capital."

Logan tipped his head. "You'll have it."

"And if Namirah opposes?"

"She is not our master."

Calim nodded to Kara. "Cousin."

Kara winced and glanced around to see if anyone had heard. "Don't call me that," she snapped. "I don't want to be drawn into this game."

"You're already playing, whether you like it or not. The game chooses its players."

Calim's contingent rode out, halving their number. The rest of them busied themselves breaking down tents and preparing to travel.

Lena lingered at the edge of the camp, eyes never leaving her son.

Kara took Logan's hand. "You should talk to her. She helped us, in the end."

Logan looked down at their joined hands and squeezed tighter. "I will. I should like to get to know her, I think. Before it's too late. Will you come with me? I'd like to introduce you."

"We met—in the dungeons. She was the one who released me the night of Victus's illusions."

A low growl hummed in the back of Logan's throat, and Kara quickly recovered. "I don't think she had a choice, Logan. Don't blame her for his machinations. She's just lost, is all. Has been for a long time."

Logan went to her, and they talked in quiet whispers on the edge of camp, an insurpassable distance between them.

Kara caught the tail end of their conversation as they walked back, a fragile smile on Lena's face.

"You may come with us, if you wish," Logan said. "Things are going to be turbulent with the Riders."

Lena shook her head. "I have a son to bury."

Logan gave a tight nod. Once again, she wasn't choosing him. "You'd be of more use to me if you stayed, anyways."

"You want me to spy?"

"Yes."

Lena's back stiffened. "I'll consider it."

There was no embrace, no parting glance as mother and son walked away from each other.

THE JOURNEY back to Raven's Rest was long and hard. Tensions were strained, and the entire party felt like a powder keg about to ignite. Wesley tried to approach Kara several times on the road, but she still wasn't ready. She had no idea what she would say to him—if she could even forgive him. His recent kindness didn't make up for all the harm he'd caused.

She was enjoying the opportunity to ride Drum again. She'd had a tearful reunion with the mare, and was lavishing her with treats and long grooming sessions to make up for their lost time together.

Many of the Stygians were uneasy around Namirah, frequently glancing between her and Kara and crossing themselves with ward signs. They gave the sorceress a wide berth, even once they were on the road.

Jon had no such qualms. "So," he said, riding up alongside Namirah and taking a crunchy bite of an apple. "How exactly are you alive, again?"

Namirah gifted him the slightest smile. "I never died to begin with. Not truly. My flesh suffered, but my soul was already half in the shadow realm from the time I bonded with my demon. When Urian's dogs finally cornered me, I knew I'd lost. I cast a spell that sent the remaining half of my soul through the veil, trapping it but preserving it. My body was essentially an animated husk at that point. They burnt my earthly shell, but they couldn't kill *me*—or my power."

"How did you communicate with Victus?" Logan asked. "How did he know he could bring you back?"

"My power from beyond the veil was limited. I could send whispers to places where my magic still lived in the earth and water—a side effect of my curse—but someone had to be listening. Victus and his blood mage listened more closely than most."

"And did you tell him to imprison and torture cursed women to harvest their power? To target Kara?" Logan growled. The spikes on his shoulders flared.

"Of course not. I love all my children. Even you, Logan Vakarian."

"I am not *yours*."

"So literal. I know my granddaughter has claimed you, beast."

"And what are your intentions for this second life you've been granted?" Rahj asked from atop his palomino.

"My time in Teleria ended too soon. I never had a chance to reverse my curse, and it has flourished…unmitigated." Her gaze slid to Logan.

"Forgive me if I suspect motives beyond altruism from you," Jon said.

"I did much harm my first time on this earth. I should like to improve with the second."

"So that's where I pulled you from?" Kara asked. "The shadow realm?"

"The realm between realms."

"Where will you go, now that you're free?"

"Wherever you go, of course. I sacrificed my relationship with your mother to keep her safe from Urian and Genevieve. I won't make the same mistake with you."

Kara stilled. The most powerful mage Teleria had ever seen, Cursebringer and Kingbreaker, and she wanted to bond.

"No ulterior motives?"

Namirah's smile glinted. "A tiger cannot change her spots."

"Tigers have stripes."

"Exactly."

Kara rolled her eyes. "At least you're honest."

The sun glinted against something on Namirah's chest, and Kara narrowed her eyes. A familiar crystal wrapped in leather strips hung from a thong around her neck. The crystal she'd brought through the portal with her—the very first thing she'd thrust into this world upon waking. Kara swallowed past the lump in her throat.

EACH NIGHT WHEN THEY CAMPED, Logan and Kara shared a tent. They made love—sometimes rough and hurried, sometimes sweet and slow—and talked of their future together. The surrounding landscape grew more familiar the closer to the Blackshear they rode. Mountains grew in the distance, and rolling hills bowed down to thick forests. When the front of their party crested the final hill before the Blackshear's border, they all whoaed their horses. A collective hush swept over them.

Unease skittered down Kara's spine. "What? What do you see?" Kara asked.

Someone raised a shaky finger to the horizon. Kara kneed Drum into a trot, moving to the top of the hill. She sucked in a breath as she crested it.

The Blackshear was a ragged wound upon the earth.

Trees, once green and proud, were the color of blood. A thick grey cloud hovered overhead, though the sky beyond its borders was clear and sunny. The forest she knew was gone. And Raven's Rest waited within.

Kara kicked Drum into a gallop.

"Wait!" Logan called, racing after her with Char.

Getting closer did nothing to allay her fears. It wasn't some foreign sap or invasive species of vine. Every piece of the trees had turned—bark, needles, leaves, flowers. Like the sky had been bleeding for weeks.

Namirah rode up to her and Logan. They stood even with each other, staring towards the crimson stain of a forest.

"The veil has opened," Namirah said.

FREE BONUS CONTENT

()

Want to read the scene of Kara's first keening from Logan's point of view?

Sign up for my newsletter at **sarasellers.com** and receive a link to this free exclusive.

I'd love it if you could leave me a review. Reviews are the lifeblood of authors like me, and they allow me to keep writing. Thank you!

COMING SOON

○

Kara and Logan's story will conclude in *Namirah's Chosen*.

Sign up for my newsletter at **sarasellers.com** to be notified when it's available for preorder.

ADVANCED READER TEAM

◯

Want to be part of my advanced reader team that receives
early access to new releases?

Sign up at **sarasellers.com/links**

ACKNOWLEDGMENTS

()

Thank you Lindsey, Mom, Dad, Grandma, and Rex for the endless encouragement. Your encouragement has been invaluable. They say the second book's the hardest—so here's to book three!

ABOUT THE AUTHOR

()

Sara Sellers lives in Georgia with her three cats. She likes the sound of rain, the smell of gasoline, and the taste of boiled peanuts. She has a soft spot in her heart for K-dramas and training montages.

Find out more at sarasellers.com
Join my reader group at facebook.com/groups/sarasellers

tiktok.com/@sellerssara

facebook.com/authorsarasellers

x.com/sellerssara

instagram.com/sellerssara

threads.net/@sellerssara

pinterest.com/sellerssara

goodreads.com/sarasellers

amazon.com/author/sarasellers

bookbub.com/authors/sara-sellers

9 781737 219439